TO:

FROM:

DATE:

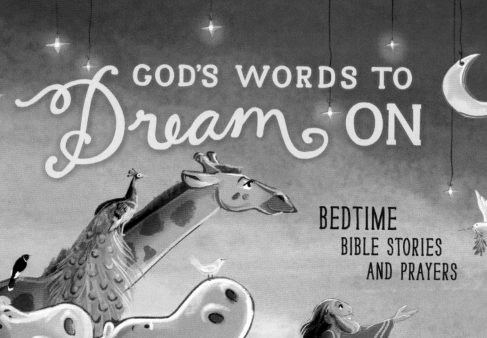

GOD'S WORDS TO
Dream ON

BEDTIME
BIBLE STORIES
AND PRAYERS

FROM THE AUTHOR OF
I AM: 40 REASONS TO TRUST GOD

Diane Stortz
Illustrated by Diane Le Feyer

An Imprint of Thomas Nelson

Published in Nashville, Tennessee, by Tommy Nelson. Tommy Nelson is an imprint of Thomas Nelson. Thomas Nelson is a registered trademark of HarperCollins Christian Publishing, Inc.

Published in association with Books & Such Literary Management, 52 Mission Circle, Suite 122, PMB 170, Santa Rosa, California 95409, www.booksandsuch.com.

Illustrated by Diane Le Feyer.

Tommy Nelson titles may be purchased in bulk for educational, business, fund-raising, or sales promotional use. For information, please email SpecialMarkets@ThomasNelson.com.

Library of Congress Cataloging-in-Publication Data is on file.

ISBN-13: 978-1-4002-0935-4

Printed in China

18 19 20 21 22 DSC 6 5 4 3 2 1

Mfr. DSC / Shenzhen, China / March 2019 / PO# 9526823

For Asher and Reed.

—DS

Contents

A Letter to Parents   6

OLD TESTAMENT STORIES

In the Beginning, God   10

Trouble in the Garden   14

Safe in a Big Boat   18

What Did You Say?   22

A Baby for Sarah   26

Isaac and Rebekah   30

Jacob's Ladder   34

Trouble for Joseph   38

Family Reunion   42

Baby in a Basket   46

At the Burning Bush   50

Pharaoh Says No   54

Safely Through the Sea   58

Food for Hungry Travelers   62

Ten Good Rules   66

Scout It Out!   70

Into the Promised Land   74

Ruth's Rich Reward   78

What Samuel Heard   82

Only a Boy Named David   86

The Small and the Tall   90

What Solomon Wanted   94

Birds and Bread   98

Jonah Runs Away   102

Daniel and the Hungry Lions   106

New Walls and a Long Wait   110

NEW TESTAMENT STORIES

One Silent Night 116

Good News for All People 120

Taller, Stronger, Wiser 124

This Is My Son 128

So Many Fish! 132

Down Through the Roof 136

Jesus Chooses Twelve 140

Wind and Sea Obey Him 144

Jesus the Healer 148

Feeding a Crowd 152

Who's the Greatest? 156

A Good Neighbor 160

The Most Important Thing 164

A Father Forgives 168

Lazarus Lives 172

Let the Children Come 176

Zacchaeus Meets Jesus 180

Remember Me 184

Sad Day, Glad Day 188

He Will Come Again 192

The Holy Spirit Comes 196

Walking and Leaping 200

Saul's Big Surprise 204

Praying for Peter 208

A Young Believer 212

Forever with Jesus 216

Create a Happy Bedtime Routine 220

Tips for Reading with Young Children 222

About the Author 224

A Letter to Parents

Dear Parents,

How satisfying it is to send a child off to dreamland feeling peaceful, content, and secure! Reading bedtime stories to children has been an important part of families' good-night routines for generations because stories bring us close, create memories, and help us communicate.

Bible stories at bedtime are often a child's first introduction to spending time with God's Word, and the effects can go deep. The apostle Paul wrote to his spiritual son Timothy, "From childhood you have been acquainted with the sacred writings, which are able to make you wise for salvation through faith in Christ Jesus" (2 Timothy 3:15).

Young children thrive on routine and ritual, and a Bible story at bedtime is one of the best!

I chose the Bible stories in *God's Words to Dream On* specifically for young children getting ready for sleep. Not only do the stories create an overview of the entire Bible from Genesis to Revelation—the story of God's plan from before creation to someday send Jesus, the One who would make things right again—but they also focus on God's loving care and His trustworthiness, power, and protection. Each includes a blessing for your child, a simple Bible verse, and a good-night prayer.

With these fifty-two stories, you can introduce your child to our loving God and His wonderful Word. Together you can experience enjoyable, positive moments at bedtime, and your child can go to sleep feeling secure in your love—and in the love of our heavenly Father and our Savior, Jesus.

Sweet dreams!

Diane Stortz

Old Testament Stories

When you lie down,
your sleep will be peaceful.
—Proverbs 3:24 ICB

In the Beginning, God

Genesis 1–2

⊷ GOD'S WORDS TO DREAM ON ⊷

In the beginning, God created the
heavens and the earth. —Genesis 1:1

Make-believe stories often begin "Once upon a time . . ." But God's *true* story
starts like this: "In the beginning, God created the heavens and the earth."
Out of nothing, God made everything. No one else could do that!

On the first five days of the beginning of everything, God created light
and darkness, the sea and the sky, and the land. He made tall trees and
bright, beautiful flowers pop up on the land. With a *plink, plink, plink,* He hung
the sun, the moon, and the stars—more stars than you could *ever* count, and
He knows each one by name! He filled the air with soaring birds and the seas
with fish and whales, dolphins and snails. On the sixth day, He formed animals of every kind to make their homes on the land, from the small bouncing
bunny to the huge hippopotamus.

God liked what He made. He saw that it was good. But He still wasn't finished. He had saved the best for last.

"It's time!" God said. "Time to make people in Our image. They will care for all the fish in the sea and the birds of the air and the animals of the land."

From the ground, God picked up some dust and used the dust to make the first man. He breathed life into the man and named him Adam. Then God planted a garden in a place called Eden. The garden was Adam's new home.

But God *still* wasn't finished.

"It isn't good for Adam to be alone," God said. "I'll make just the right helper and friend for him." First, God brought the birds and animals to Adam and let Adam name each one. But none of the birds or animals was the helper and friend he needed. Then God used one of Adam's ribs to make a woman, Eve, and He brought her to Adam to be his wife.

"At last!" Adam said.

Now God's work was done. All He had made was *very good*, and He blessed Adam and Eve. "Have children and grand-children, and fill the earth," God said. "Take care of the earth and all the birds and fish and animals."

On the seventh day of the beginning of everything, God rested and enjoyed all He had made—a beautiful world for you!

✦ SLEEPY-TIME PRAYER ✦

Dear God, thank You for making our wonderful world and everything in it. Thank You for making me and all the people I love. Good night, God! Amen.

BEDTIME BLESSING

God made a wonderful world for you.

13

Trouble in the Garden

Genesis 2–3

❧ GOD'S WORDS TO DREAM ON ❧

His faithful love endures forever.
—1 Chronicles 16:34 NLT

Adam and Eve
lived happily in
God's splendid garden
until the day a sneaky
snake—who was really Satan—
decided to cause trouble.

Two special trees grew in the garden, the tree of knowing good and evil and the tree of living forever. The sneaky snake asked Eve, "Did God *really* tell you not to eat the fruit from any tree in the garden?"

It was a trick question! Adam and Eve could eat the fruit from every tree in the garden *except* the tree of knowing good and evil. This was God's rule.

Adam knew the rule.

And Eve knew the rule.

"Oh no," said Eve. "We can eat the fruit from every tree *except* the tree of knowing good and evil. God said we will die if we eat from that tree."

Now, the sneaky snake knew God's rule too. And he knew God's words are always true. But the snake wanted to hurt Adam and Eve.

"You won't die," the snake lied. "You'll be like God, that's all, knowing good and evil."

Eve looked at the tree and its beautiful fruit. Would the fruit taste yummy? Would God care if she tried just a little? And being like God seemed a good idea. So Eve picked a piece of fruit and took a bite. She gave some to Adam, and he ate the fruit too.

Oh, but doing what God said not to do was quite a *bad* idea! As soon as Adam and Eve ate the fruit, a deep sadness settled in their hearts, and they tried to hide from God the next time He called to them.

Adam blamed Eve, and Eve blamed the snake.

God punished the snake, and Adam and Eve could no longer eat from the tree of living forever—they had to leave the beautiful garden.

But God would never stop loving Adam and Eve. And God had a plan. One day He would send Someone to make everything right again.

✎ SLEEPY-TIME PRAYER ✎

Dear God, thank You for loving me. Thank You for teaching me what is wrong and what is right. I'm glad You never stop loving me! Good night, God! Amen.

BEDTIME BLESSING

God never stops loving you.

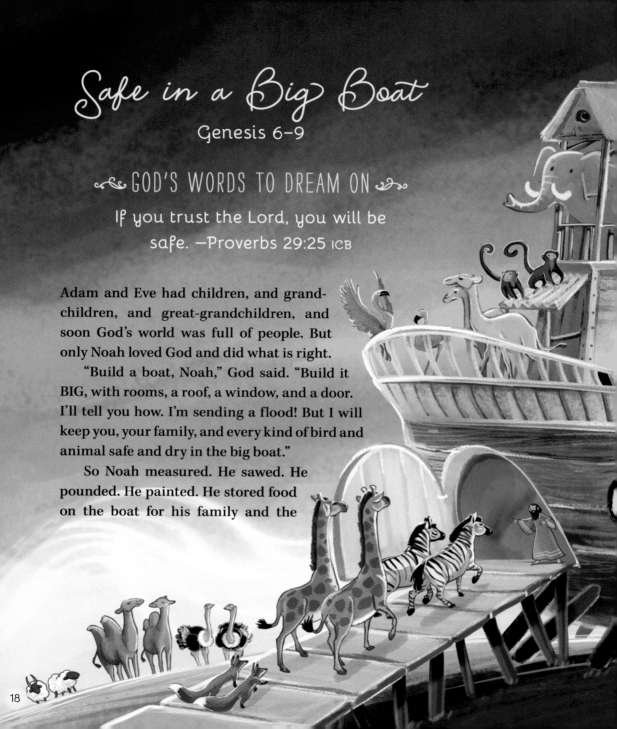

Safe in a Big Boat

Genesis 6–9

⚬∾ GOD'S WORDS TO DREAM ON ∾⚬

If you trust the Lord, you will be safe. —Proverbs 29:25 ICB

Adam and Eve had children, and grand-children, and great-grandchildren, and soon God's world was full of people. But only Noah loved God and did what is right.

"Build a boat, Noah," God said. "Build it BIG, with rooms, a roof, a window, and a door. I'll tell you how. I'm sending a flood! But I will keep you, your family, and every kind of bird and animal safe and dry in the big boat."

So Noah measured. He sawed. He pounded. He painted. He stored food on the boat for his family and the

animals. When the work was done, God said, "Go into the boat with your wife and your sons and their wives too, and take in the animals and birds I send to you."

Then pairs of every kind of bird and animal came to the boat and went inside with Noah and his family. When everyone was on board, God closed the door.

Noah, his family, and the birds and animals waited. But not for long!

~ BEDTIME BLESSING ~
You are always safe with God.

20

Drip . . . drop. Drip, drip, drop! Splish-splash, pitter-patter, drip-drip-DROP! For forty days, the rain poured down. Noah's big boat began to float. Water covered all the land. But inside the boat, everyone stayed safe and dry, just as God had promised.

When the rain stopped, Noah sent out a dove. The dove brought back an olive leaf—a sign that the land was drying out! Soon God told Noah, "Go out of the boat with your wife and your sons and their wives and all the birds and animals I sent to you."

Everyone came out of the boat and stood on the good, dry land. Noah built an altar to thank God for taking care of them during the flood.

"Start new homes all over the earth," God said. "Have children and grandchildren. I will never send another flood like this one. And every rainbow in the sky will remind you of My promise."

⚘ SLEEPY-TIME PRAYER ⚘

Dear God, thank You for keeping me safe,
day and night! Thank You for Your rainbow
promise. Good night, God! Amen.

What Did You Say?

Genesis 11

❧ GOD'S WORDS TO DREAM ON ❧

Everything the Lord does is
right. —Psalm 145:17 ICB

All the people on earth spoke the same language. Every person could understand every other person, which was a fine thing, except that people mostly talked about how great *they* were—they didn't think they needed God at all.

And the people didn't care that God had said, "Start new homes all over the earth." In fact, they decided they would *not* spread out all over the earth. "Come on, everyone!" they said to one another. "Let's build a great city for ourselves, right here, all together. And let's build a tower in the city, a tower so tall it goes higher than the clouds. We can do it because we are amazing! And we'll all stay together, right where we are."

So the people got busy. They made bricks and started building. They started building the city and a *very* tall tower.

Now, what do you think God said about that?

"The people are very proud of themselves," God said. "They all speak the same language, and they all want to stay in one place instead of spreading out over the earth as I told them to do. They think they don't need Me."

But God had a plan. "Here's what we will do," God said. "We will go down and confuse their language. They won't be able to understand one another anymore. Then they will have to leave their city and spread out over the earth."

So God mixed up the people's language. Everyone couldn't understand everyone else anymore. Instead, they kept asking each other, "What? What? What did you say?" But that didn't help.

Because they couldn't understand each other anymore, the people stopped building the city. They called the city Babel, which means "confused." They left the city and began to live all over the earth, just as God had told them to do.

⤳ SLEEPY-TIME PRAYER ⤲

Dear God, I want to do what You say.
Thank You for teaching me and helping
me obey. Good night, God! Amen.

BEDTIME BLESSING

God's ways are always best for you.

A Baby for Sarah

Genesis 12; 15; 17–18; 21

❧ GOD'S WORDS TO DREAM ON ❧

The Lord's plans stand firm
forever. —Psalm 33:11 NLT

Before God made the world, He planned an amazing plan. One day, at just the right time, He would send His Son, Jesus, to earth. But first He had to get the world ready for that special day.

God chose a man named Abraham. He promised to give Abraham new land and a big family. "I'm going to begin a new nation," God said. "I'm going to bless you so you can be a blessing to everyone in the whole world!"

Abraham wondered how God would give him a big family because he and his wife, Sarah, were quite old and didn't have *any* children at all! So Abraham asked God about it.

"Look up at the stars," God told Abraham. "Can you count them all? No, there are too many to count. That's how big your family will be."

Abraham believed God, and God was pleased with him.

Years passed. When Abraham was ninety-nine, God came to Abraham and said, "At this time next year, your wife, Sarah, will have a baby boy. Name him Isaac. I will bless Isaac and give him My promises, just as I have given them to you."

Abraham fell down laughing when he heard such happy news! He would be one hundred years old when the baby was born, and Sarah would be ninety. How could people so old have a baby? That seemed impossible to him, but Abraham knew that God could make it happen.

A little later, three men from God came to visit Abraham as he sat outside his tent near a big oak tree. Abraham and Sarah fixed a special meal for their guests. While they were eating, one of the men said, "This time next year, I will come to visit you again, and Sarah will have a baby boy."

Sarah was listening from inside the tent. She laughed to herself and thought, *Could I really have a baby? I'm so old!*

God knew that Sarah had laughed, and He said, "Is anything too hard for the Lord?"

God kept His promise to Abraham and Sarah. He gave them a baby boy even though they both were old. They called the baby Isaac, the name God had chosen.

"Everyone is smiling and laughing with me now!" Sarah said. "Abraham and I have a son!"

◦◦ SLEEPY-TIME PRAYER ◦◦

Dear God, You had plans for Abraham and Sarah, and You have plans for me. Show me how to follow Your plans, now and when I'm all grown up. Good night, God! Amen.

Isaac and Rebekah

Genesis 24

❧ GOD'S WORDS TO DREAM ON ☙

He will guide us forever. —Psalm 48:14

Isaac grew up. Abraham wanted Isaac to have a good wife. Abraham said to his servant, "Go to the land where my relatives live, and find a wife for Isaac. God will guide you."

The servant loaded up ten camels with presents for Abraham's relatives and supplies for the trip. Then he set off toward the place where Abraham's relatives lived. When he got close, he stopped at a well so the camels could get a drink. He waited for someone to come to draw water out of the well, and as he waited, he prayed. "Oh, Lord, show Your love for Abraham, and help me today," he said. "Let the young woman who gives me a drink and offers to get water for my camels be the one You have chosen to be Isaac's wife."

Before the servant finished his prayer, Rebekah came to the well with a water jar on her shoulder.

"Please give me a drink," the servant said.

"Gladly, sir," Rebekah said. "And I will get water for your camels too!" Rebekah filled the trough with water for the thirsty camels.

Abraham's servant gave Rebekah a shiny gold ring and two gold bracelets. Then he asked Rebekah about her father. "My father's name is Bethuel," Rebekah said.

Bethuel was Abraham's relative! "God has been faithful and loving to Abraham and to me!" the servant said. "He has led me here to Abraham's relatives!"

⌁ SLEEPY-TIME PRAYER ⌁

Dear God, thank You for being the guide for my life. I want to follow You. Good night, God! Amen.

Abraham's servant told Rebekah's family all about Abraham, Sarah, and their son, Isaac. He told them about his journey and what he had prayed while he waited at the well. "God answered my prayer," he said. "Rebekah came to the well and gave me a drink, and she offered to give my camels a drink too."

Rebekah's relatives said, "Yes, God guided you here!"

In the morning, Rebecca's mother and brother asked her, "Do you want to marry Isaac?"

Rebekah said yes. So she rode one of the servant's camels back to the land where Abraham and Isaac lived. She became Isaac's wife, and Isaac loved her.

~ BEDTIME BLESSING ~
God will always guide you.

Jacob's Ladder

Genesis 25–26; 28

❧ GOD'S WORDS TO DREAM ON ❧

"I will not leave you." —Joshua 1:5 ICB

God gave Isaac and Rebekah two baby boys—twins named Esau and Jacob. Even though they were twins, they didn't look alike, and they didn't act alike. In fact, as they got older, Jacob and Esau sometimes argued. But God had a plan for each of them. The promises God had given to Abraham, He also had given to the twins' father, Isaac, and soon God would give the promises to Jacob too.

Isaac sent Jacob on a journey back to the land of Abraham's relatives to find a young woman to marry. When the sun went down, Jacob stopped to spend the night. He found a flat stone and put it under his head like a pillow. Soon he was fast asleep, and he began to dream.

In his dream, Jacob saw a ladder reaching from earth to heaven, with angels going up and down the ladder. What do you think those angels looked like?

God stood at the top of the ladder, and as Jacob dreamed, he heard God talking to him! What do you think God said?

I am the God of your grandfather Abraham and your father, Isaac," God told Jacob. "I will give all this land to you, to your children and grandchildren, and to their children and grandchildren. Your family will be too big to be counted, and I will bless everyone on earth through you. I am with you, and I will take care of you wherever you go, and I will bring you back to this land. I will not leave you."

The dream ended. Jacob woke up. "Surely the Lord is here with me," Jacob said, "and I didn't know it!"

⌘ BEDTIME BLESSING ⌘

God is with you
everywhere you go.

Early in the morning, Jacob took the stone that had been his pillow and stood it up on one end to remind him of his dream. "Go with me on this journey, Lord," he prayed. "Take care of me and give me what I need, and bring me back this way again. And I will follow and worship You." Then Jacob continued walking toward the land of Abraham's relatives.

SLEEPY-TIME PRAYER

Dear God, thank You for loving me and taking care of me everywhere I go. You're even with me when I'm asleep! Good night, God! Amen.

Trouble for Joseph

Genesis 37; 39; 41

⋅⋗ GOD'S WORDS TO DREAM ON ⋖⋅

"Don't be afraid. I will help you." —Isaiah 41:13 ICB

Jacob got married and had twelve sons. He lived with his sons in the land of Canaan. One of Jacob's sons, Joseph, had a special coat to wear, which made his brothers jealous. And Joseph sometimes tattled on his brothers, which made them mad.

"Listen to this dream I had," Joseph said one day. "I dreamed that we

were all gathering wheat in the field, and my bundle of wheat stood up, and your bundles of wheat bowed down to mine."

"Do you think you will rule over us?" Joseph's brothers asked.

Then Joseph had another dream. "I dreamed that the sun, the moon, and eleven stars all bowed down to me," he said.

"Do you think we will all bow down to you?" Jacob asked. And Joseph's brothers felt even angrier with Joseph than they had before.

One day Jacob sent Joseph to check on his brothers, who were caring for the family's sheep. "Here comes that dreamer!" the brothers said. "Let's grab him and throw him in a pit."

Poor Joseph! He probably felt scared and alone. But God was with him.

Soon the brothers saw some traders on their way to Egypt. "I've got an idea," one brother said. "Let's pull Joseph out of the pit and sell him to those traders. They will take him to Egypt, and we won't have to put up with him any longer." More trouble for Joseph! But God was with him.

In Egypt, Joseph worked for a man named Potiphar, and everything Joseph did for Potiphar turned out well. But one day, even though Joseph hadn't done anything wrong, Potiphar became angry with Joseph and threw him into prison.

More trouble for Joseph! But God was with Joseph even in prison. Joseph worked hard, and everything he did turned out well. And God gave Joseph the ability to understand dreams. When the king of Egypt had a puzzling dream, someone told him about Joseph. "Bring Joseph here right now!" the king said.

So Joseph got out of prison. He got a bath, a haircut, and new clothes. Then he went to see the king, wondering what would happen next.

~ BEDTIME BLESSING ~
Even if bad things happen,
God is with you.

~ SLEEPY-TIME PRAYER ~
Dear God, thank You for always being with me, in good times and bad times. I'm so glad You're there to help me all the time! Good night, God! Amen.

Family Reunion

Genesis 41–42; 45–46; 50

Give thanks to the LORD, for he
is good. —Psalm 136:1

Joseph came to see Pharaoh, the king of Egypt. "Can you tell me what my dreams mean?" Pharaoh asked Joseph.

"God knows what they mean," Joseph said. "So tell me your dreams, and God will show me what they mean."

"First I dreamed that seven skinny cows on the bank of the Nile River swallowed seven plump cows," Pharaoh said. "Then I dreamed that seven skinny heads of grain on one stalk swallowed seven plump ears of grain."

"God gave you the dreams to tell you what is surely going to happen," Joseph said. "First will come seven good years, when more than enough grain will grow.

After that will come seven bad years, when no grain will grow. Find someone wise to be in charge of storing up grain during the seven good years. When the seven bad years come, people can eat the grain that has been stored up."

"You are the wise man for the job," Pharaoh said. "I'm putting you in charge of all the land of Egypt."

After all the bad things that had happened to him, Joseph probably felt happy to hear that! He did his job well, and when the seven bad years began, Joseph had stored up plenty of grain. People from all over Egypt and other lands came to Joseph to buy it. Even Joseph's brothers came, because people in the land of Canaan needed food too.

Joseph's brothers didn't recognize him. But Joseph recognized them, and he remembered his dreams from long before. He

BEDTIME BLESSING
God makes everything
work out for good.

44

didn't tell his brothers who he was right away. He waited to find out whether they had become more honest and kindhearted.

Later he said, "My brothers! I am Joseph, the one you sold to traders! I rule over Egypt now. God sent me here ahead of you to store up food to keep you all alive. You meant to harm me, but God meant it for good. Go now and bring our father, Jacob, and your families to live in Egypt."

So Jacob, Joseph's brothers, and all their families moved from Canaan to Egypt. Together again, they lived there in peace for many years.

SLEEPY-TIME PRAYER

Dear God, I give You thanks because You're
good! You make everything turn out right.
I love You, God. Good night! Amen.

Baby in a Basket

Exodus 1–2

Tell all the nations, "The LORD
reigns!" —Psalm 96:10 NLT

In Egypt, God was making the family of Abraham, Isaac, and Jacob into a large nation, just as He had promised. Jacob's big family got even bigger. The people were known as Hebrews.

Then one day Egypt got a new king. This pharaoh didn't know anything about Joseph, his father, or his brothers. This pharaoh thought there were too many Hebrews in Egypt. "From now on, the Hebrews will be slaves!" Pharaoh said. "They must make bricks, build buildings, and work in the fields."

But the number of Hebrews kept growing. So Pharaoh made another bad decision. He told the Hebrew mommies to throw their boy babies into the Nile River!

One mommy, Jochebed, didn't do what Pharaoh wanted. She hid her baby boy at home, but after three months he was too big—and too noisy!—to hide any longer. Jochebed thought about what to do. She made a basket just the baby's size and painted it with tar so it would float. Then she

put the baby in the basket and placed the basket among the grasses grow-ing at the side of the river. Miriam, the baby's sister, hid nearby to see what would happen.

Soon the princess of Egypt came to the river to take a bath. "Look at that basket!" the princess said. She sent one of her servants to bring her the basket, and when she opened it, she found the baby inside, crying.

"This is one of the Hebrew babies," the princess said. She wanted to keep the baby and help him, but how would she feed him?

~~~ BEDTIME BLESSING ~~~
God is always in charge.

Miriam ran to the princess. "Would you like me to find a Hebrew woman who can nurse the baby for you?" she asked.

"Yes, please!" the princess said.

So Miriam ran home and told Jochebed what had happened. She brought Jochebed, the baby's very own mother, to the princess.

"I will take the baby home and take care of him for you," Jochebed said with joy in her heart.

Later, when her son was older, Jochebed brought him to the princess. "I will call him Moses," the princess said.

So Moses, a Hebrew child, grew up in Pharaoh's palace.

⟳ SLEEPY-TIME PRAYER ⟲

Dear God, nothing bad can stop Your good plans.
You took care of Moses, and You take care of
me. Thank You, God! Good night! Amen.

At the Burning Bush

Exodus 2–4

⮜⮜ GOD'S WORDS TO DREAM ON ⮞⮞

The Lord listens when I pray
to him. —Psalm 4:3 ICB

Moses grew up in Pharaoh's palace, but he knew he was a Hebrew. One day he left the palace and became a shepherd in the desert. The Hebrews still worked hard every day as slaves in Egypt. They wanted to be rescued from their slavery!

God saw what was happening, and He would help them.

One day in the desert, near a mountain, Moses saw a strange sight—a bush on fire but not burning up! Moses wanted to find out what was happening, so he went closer. That's when he heard a voice calling from the bush, "Moses! Moses!"

Moses didn't see anyone. Who was calling him? "Here I am," Moses said.

God was calling Moses! "Take off your sandals," God said, "because this is a holy place. I am the God of your father, and the God of Abraham, Isaac, and Jacob. I know My people are being badly treated. I am sending you to lead them out of Egypt and into the good land I promised them. I want you to visit Pharaoh and tell him to let My people go."

"But how can I do a big job like that?" Moses asked. "That's too hard for me."

"I will be with you, Moses," God said. "You will bring My people out of Egypt and lead them here, to worship Me near this mountain. Now go, and tell my people I am the God of their fathers—Abraham, Isaac, and Jacob. Tell them I have heard their cries and I will rescue them. Pharaoh will not want to let them go, but I will do wonders in Egypt, and finally he will let them go."

"But what if the people don't believe me?" Moses asked.

"I will help you do special signs with your shepherd's staff," God said.

"But I'm not a good speaker," Moses said. "How can I talk to Your people and to Pharaoh?"

~ BEDTIME BLESSING ~
God hears you when
you ask for help.

"Your brother, Aaron, is a good speaker," God said. "He will help you. I will teach you both what to do."

Moses obeyed God. He went back to Egypt. On the way, he met his brother, Aaron. Together they went to talk to God's people. "God is going to help you and bring you out of Egypt," they said.

When the people heard the good news, they bowed their heads and worshipped God.

⟞ SLEEPY-TIME PRAYER ⟝

Dear God, thank You for listening to me when
I pray. You're listening to me right now! I'm glad
I can talk to You. Good night, God! Amen.

Pharaoh Says No

Exodus 5–12

⊱ GOD'S WORDS TO DREAM ON ⊰

Your word is like a lamp for
my feet and a light for my
way. —Psalm 119:105 ICB

Moses and Aaron went to Pharaoh with God's message. "God says, 'Let My people go!'" they told him.

Pharaoh said, "No! You can't go. I'm in charge here, not God. Tell the people to get back to work making bricks and building buildings." Pharaoh made the people work even harder than before.

The people blamed Moses and Aaron. "See what has happened to us now!" they shouted. But God knew how He would rescue His people.

"I am the Lord," God told Moses. "Wait to see what I will do. I know Pharaoh will not listen to you. But I will send trouble to Egypt, signs that will change his mind. Everyone in Egypt will know I am the Lord."

First, God changed the water in the Nile River to blood. No one could drink it!

Pharaoh didn't care. "No!" he said. "The people can't go."

Then frogs swarmed everywhere in the houses of the Egyptians—even in their beds and baking bowls!

But Pharaoh said, "No! The people can't go."

God sent swarms of teeny-tiny gnats buzzing around in the cities and fields of Egypt, and after that He sent swarms of flies. Then cattle got sick.

BEDTIME BLESSING

God will make
a way for you.

Pharaoh said, "No! The people can't go."

The Egyptians got painful sores on their skin. A terrible storm ruined their crops. An army of locusts ate what was left. Then came thick darkness for three days. But where the Hebrews lived, nothing bad happened. God kept His people safe. Still, Pharaoh said, "No, no, no! The people can't go!"

Finally, one sad night, many Egyptians died. But God kept all the Hebrews safe. Pharaoh gave up. He changed his "No! No! No!" to "Go! Go! Go!"

Moses and all the Hebrews packed up quickly and hurried out of Egypt.

❧ SLEEPY-TIME PRAYER ☙

Dear God, when something seems hard, help
me remember that You will make a way!
I love You, God. Good night! Amen.

Safely Through the Sea
Exodus 12–15

❧ GOD'S WORDS TO DREAM ON ❧

Every word of God proves
true. —Proverbs 30:5

The Hebrews, who were also called the Israelites, followed Moses out of Egypt with their children and their sheep, cattle, and goats. God had promised to take them to a new land, and He showed them the way. During the daytime He led them with a pillar of cloud, and at night the cloud was filled with bright fire, which gave the people light. Soon the people camped near the Red Sea.

But back in Egypt, Pharaoh had changed his mind. "I shouldn't have let those people go!" he said. He got his chariot ready and set out with his army to find the Israelites and bring them back.

The people could see Pharaoh and his powerful army coming toward them when the army was still far away. Maybe they heard the sound of the army's chariots pounding across the desert sand. "Oh no!" the people cried out to Moses. "The Egyptians are coming, and we're trapped here beside the Red Sea. What will we do?"

"Don't be afraid!" Moses said. "The Lord will save you. The Lord will fight for you! Just wait quietly."

The sounds of Pharaoh's army got louder. The Israelites trembled, but they tried to stay calm as Moses said to do. The pillar of cloud and fire moved between the Israelites and the Egyptians. Then God told Moses, "Stretch out your staff over the sea. The water

will part, and everyone will walk through the sea on dry ground."

Moses obeyed God, and God sent a strong wind to part the water and make a dry path for the people to walk on. Everyone walked through the sea with a wall of water on each side!

Pharaoh and his army chased the Israelites right into the sea. But in the morning God made the Egyptians' chariot wheels twist and stick. "Let's get out of here!" Pharaoh's men cried. They tried to turn around and go back.

When the Israelites reached the other side, God told Moses to stretch out his hand over the sea once more. The walls of water came crashing down on Pharaoh and his army.

Hurrah! The Israelites celebrated God's great power and what God had done for them. He had brought them out of Egypt and

saved them from Pharaoh's army! The women danced, and Moses sang with all the people, "God, there is no one else like You! You do great miracles! You keep Your loving promises, and You will lead and guide us to a new land!"

⌁ SLEEPY-TIME PRAYER ⌁

Dear God, I'm glad I know that You will always do what You say. Thank You for Your words and promises. Good night, God! Amen.

⌁ BEDTIME BLESSING ⌁

God keeps His promises.

Food for Hungry Travelers

Exodus 16

❧ GOD'S WORDS TO DREAM ON ☙

He gives food to every living
creature. —Psalm 136:25 ICB

God led Moses and the Israelites through the wilderness. But soon they began to forget how God had rescued them from Egypt.

"We're *hungry*," the people whined to Moses and Aaron. "When we were back in Egypt, we had plenty of food. What are we going to eat out here in the wilderness?"

Moses asked God about the problem.

"I'm going to send the people bread from heaven," God said. "Tell them to get ready. I will find out if they are willing to listen to Me and obey My instructions."

"God is going to take care of you," Moses told the people. "Stop grumbling at us. Tonight you will eat meat, and in the morning you will have bread."

That evening a large flock of quail flew into the camp. The Israelites caught and roasted the quail for dinner. *Mmm.* And in the morning when they looked outside their tents, the people saw white flakes covering the ground. What was it?

"This is the bread God has sent you," Moses said. "Each of you may gather as much as you can eat today. Don't save any leftovers. There will be more tomorrow."

The flakes tasted sweet, like wafers with honey. The Israelites called the flakes *manna*. They could bake bread with it or make hot cereal.

~ BEDTIME BLESSING ~

God will give you what you need.

64

But some people didn't listen to God's instructions. They kept leftovers in their tents that night. But the next morning, the leftovers were full of worms! *Eew!*

On the sixth day, Moses said, "This morning you will find enough manna for today *and* tomorrow. God won't send manna tomorrow because that's a special day for rest. You may gather extra manna today and save the leftovers. Tomorrow your leftovers will still be good to eat." Some people didn't listen to God's instructions. They got up the next morning and went looking for manna. But there wasn't any.

God sent manna until the people came to Canaan, the land God had promised to Abraham, Isaac, and Jacob. "Put some manna in a special jar," God told them, "to remind you and your children how I gave you food when you lived in the wilderness."

⤳ SLEEPY-TIME PRAYER ⤳

Dear God, thank You for giving me food
to eat! Thank You for giving me everything
I need. Good night, God! Amen.

Ten Good Rules

Exodus 19–20; 24; 31

❧ GOD'S WORDS TO DREAM ON ❧

How precious is your steadfast
love, O God! —Psalm 36:7

66

Before God could take the Israelites into the Promised Land, He needed to teach them how He wanted them to live. God loved the Israelites, and He wanted them to know and love Him too.

While the people were camped near Mount Sinai, God told Moses, "Tell the people to listen to Me and obey My words. Then they will be My special treasure and be a blessing to the world."

Moses told the people what God had said.

"We will do everything God tells us," the people answered.

God had a surprise for everyone too. "Tell the people I will visit them," He said to Moses. "In three days I will come down on the mountain and talk with you, and all the people will hear My voice." Everyone got ready.

On the morning of the third day, a thick cloud covered the top of the mountain. The people saw lightning. They heard thunder—*BOOM!*—and the sound of a loud trumpet blast. Moses led the people out of the camp to meet God. They listened as God spoke to them.

"I am the Lord your God," He said. "I brought you out of Egypt." He gave them ten good rules. This is what He said:

1. Worship God only.
2. God is your Creator. Do not make idols or worship them.
3. Honor God's name.
4. Rest from work on the seventh day.
5. Honor your father and mother.
6. Don't murder anyone.
7. Be faithful to your husband or wife.
8. Don't take what belongs to other people.
9. Don't lie about other people.
10. Don't be jealous of what other people have.

When the people heard God's voice and saw the lightning and smoke rising from the top of the mountain, they trembled. But Moses told them, "Don't be afraid. God wants you to know who He is so you will live right."

God called Moses to climb up the mountain. He wrote the ten good rules on two stone tablets for Moses to take back to the people.

◈ SLEEPY-TIME PRAYER ◈

Dear God, I want to know You better every day!
Thank You for giving us Your words and Your rules.
Thank You for Your love. Good night, God! Amen.

God wants you to know Him well because He loves you.

Scout It Out!

Numbers 13–14

⌒∾ GOD'S WORDS TO DREAM ON ∾⌒

Trust in the Lord with all your
heart. —Proverbs 3:5

While the Israelites camped near Canaan, the Promised Land, God told Moses, "Send twelve men to scout out the land to see what it is like."

So Moses chose twelve men, one from each tribe. "Explore the land. Then come back and tell us what you see. Do many people live there? Do the cities have walls? Are the people strong or weak? Does the land grow good crops? Be brave, explore, and bring back some crops from the land."

The twelve scouts went into Canaan and explored the land. After forty days, they came back to the camp with the biggest cluster of grapes anyone had ever seen and some pomegranates and figs. "We saw good land, with good crops," the scouts said. "But the people in the land are strong and very tall, and their cities have walls."

Only two of the scouts, Caleb and Joshua, trusted God to give the land to the Israelites just as He had promised. The other scouts said, "The people living in the land are too much for us! They're too strong and tall. We felt like grasshoppers compared to them."

When the people heard the scouts' report, they cried and grumbled. They forgot about God's promise and power. They even talked about going back to Egypt. Moses and Aaron couldn't believe it!

"Calm down!" Joshua and Caleb told the people. "The land is a good land. If God is pleased with us, He will bring us into the land and give it to us. Don't be afraid. Obey God. Let's go into the new land, for God is with us."

~~~ BEDTIME BLESSING ~~~
You can trust and obey God.

But the people wouldn't listen. They even wanted to hurt Joshua and Caleb.

What a sad day! The people didn't trust God, so He couldn't take them into the land. "I will forgive the people," God told Moses. "I will always love them. But I have shown them My power and My care many times. Because they will not trust Me and obey, the people will live in the wilderness for forty more years. Then only Caleb and Joshua, who believed My promise, will go into the land."

⤳ SLEEPY-TIME PRAYER ⤳

Dear God, Your words are true, and You keep Your promises. Help me to trust You and obey. Good night, God! Amen.

73

Into the Promised Land

Joshua 1–6

❧ GOD'S WORDS TO DREAM ON ❧

He kept every promise he had
made. —Joshua 21:45 ICB

After Moses, Joshua became the next leader of the Israelites. "Lead My people into the land I promised them," God told Joshua. "I will be with you, just as I was with Moses. I will never leave you. Be strong and very brave!"

Joshua obeyed God. The people crossed the Jordan River and went into the Promised Land. They camped near the river. Then they looked up and saw the city of Jericho, with strong stone walls and tall locked gates. "What should we do now?" Joshua wondered.

Suddenly, Joshua saw someone standing near him, holding a gleaming sword. God had sent an angel, the commander of the Lord's army, to tell Joshua what to do.

"March around the city with the priests and the soldiers every day for six days," the angel said. "The priests will sound their trumpets while you march. On the seventh day, march around the city seven times. Then the priests will blow one *long* trumpet blast, and the people will shout! The walls of Jericho will tumble down."

The angel's instructions probably sounded odd to Joshua and the people. How could marching around the city like that do any good? But marching was what God wanted the Israelites to do, so they obeyed God and did what the angel said.

Left, right, left, right. Joshua led the priests and the soldiers in a march around the city, and then they went back to their camp. They did this for six days.

On the seventh day, just as the sun came up, the march began again— one, two, three, four, five, six, seven times! Then the priests blew *long* on their trumpets, and Joshua yelled, "Now shout, for the Lord has given you the city!" Everyone shouted.

Then the city gates rattled. The city walls shook. With a *r-r-rumble* and a *t-t-tumble*, the gates and walls crashed down.

Hurrah! God had made a way for His people to keep going forward into the Promised Land, their new home.

BEDTIME BLESSING
God will lead you.

SLEEPY-TIME PRAYER

Dear God, You're so strong and mighty, and so good! I want to tell others about how wonderful You are. Good night, God! Amen.

Ruth's Rich Reward

The Book of Ruth

He rewards those who seek him. —Hebrews 11:6

78

In the land of Moab, an Israelite widow named Naomi was starting out on a journey home to Bethlehem. Before she left, she said good-bye to her Moabite daughters-in-law, Ruth and Orpah.

But Ruth didn't want to be separated from Naomi. Ruth's husband had died, so Ruth told Naomi, "I want to go with you to Bethlehem. I will go wherever you go. Your people will be my people, and your God will be my God." Ruth trusted God to take care of her and Naomi.

"All right then, my daughter," Naomi said.

Ruth and Naomi walked to Bethlehem together. They found a house to live in, but they needed food too. "I'll go to the barley fields and walk behind the workers," Ruth said. "I'll pick up grain the workers drop." God's law said that poor people were allowed to gather grain this way. When Ruth brought the grain home to Naomi, she would use it for baking bread.

The barley fields belonged to a man named Boaz, one of Naomi's relatives. Boaz came to his fields and saw Ruth working there. "Who is that?" he asked his workers.

"Her name is Ruth," the workers said. "She's the Moabite woman who came to Bethlehem with Naomi. She has been working hard all day."

Boaz talked with Ruth. "I know how kind you've been to Naomi," he said, "and how you are trusting God to care for you. God will reward you. Now, stay in my fields. Don't go anywhere else. You will be safe here, and you can pick up as much grain as you'd like."

Ruth told Naomi what Boaz had said. Naomi smiled. She had an idea about what might happen next. And Naomi was right! Soon Boaz and Ruth were married!

Later on, Ruth and Boaz had a baby boy. They named him Obed. Naomi laughed with joy when she held baby Obed.

~ BEDTIME BLESSING ~
You please God
by trusting Him.

When Obed grew up, he became the grandfather of Israel's great King David. And from David's family would come the One God had promised long ago that He would send—the One who would make everything in God's world right again.

God richly rewarded Ruth, a Moabite woman, for her kindness and her trust in Him.

⊷ SLEEPY-TIME PRAYER ⊷

Dear God, I want to trust You and please You like Ruth did! Thank You for the good things You give us when we trust You. Good night, God! Amen.

What Samuel Heard

1 Samuel 1–3

⟿ GOD'S WORDS TO DREAM ON ⟾

Hear the word of the LORD. —Jeremiah 2:4

Samuel's mother, Hannah, had prayed for him before he was born. "God, please let me have a baby," she said. "If You do, he will serve You all his life." When Samuel was old enough, he helped Eli the priest take care of the tabernacle, the beautiful tent where the Israelites worshipped God.

One night as Samuel lay in bed, he heard someone calling his name. *It must be Eli*, Samuel thought. So Samuel ran to Eli's room and said, "Here I am, Eli, for you called me."

"No, I didn't call you," Eli said. "Go back and lie down."

Samuel went back to his own place and lay down again.

"Samuel!"

Samuel heard someone calling him again. He got up and ran to Eli. "Here I am," he said, "for you called me."

Eli shook his head. "No, I didn't call you," he said. "Go back and lie down."

Samuel went back to his own place and lay down again.

"Samuel, Samuel!"

Oh, someone was calling him again! It had to be Eli. Samuel got up and ran to Eli. "Here I am," he said, "for you called me."

Eli knew he hadn't been calling Samuel. So who *was* calling him? Then Eli understood that *God* was the One calling Samuel! "Go back and lie down," Eli said. "If God calls you again, say, 'Speak, Lord, for Your servant is listening.'"

Samuel obeyed Eli. He went back to his own place and lay down. And he listened.

"Samuel!" he heard again.

"Speak, Lord, for Your servant is listening," Samuel said to God.

~ BEDTIME BLESSING ~
God has words
for you to hear.

God gave Samuel a message for Eli. In the morning, Samuel gave Eli God's message.

From that day on, Samuel kept getting to know God better, and God had important work for Samuel to do. Samuel became God's prophet and a leader for God's people, and all of Samuel's messages from God came true.

Samuel listened to God and obeyed and served Him all his life, just as Hannah, his mother, had prayed.

◄ SLEEPY-TIME PRAYER ◄

Dear God, Your messages are important! I want to listen to You and hear Your words. Good night, God! Amen.

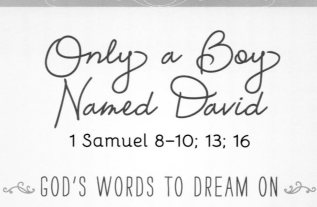

Only a Boy Named David

1 Samuel 8–10; 13; 16

❧ GOD'S WORDS TO DREAM ON ❧

Love the Lord your God with all your heart. —Deuteronomy 6:5 ICB

When the Israelites first lived in the Promised Land, they didn't have a human king—God was their King. God gave the people judges and messengers called prophets, like Samuel, to lead them. But the Israelites wanted to be like other nations. They forgot that God was their King, and they wanted someone else, a king they could see.

God gave them a king. His name was Saul. If Saul had obeyed God, he could have been a good king. But Saul didn't love God with all his heart. He didn't care about obeying God.

God wanted His people to have a good king. So God told Samuel, "Go to Bethlehem. I have chosen someone to be the next king. He is one of Jesse's sons. When you get there, I will show you who he is."

Samuel went to Bethlehem to visit Jesse and his sons. "I'm having a special dinner," Samuel said. "I want you to come."

When Jesse and his sons came to dinner, Samuel saw Jesse's son Eliab, handsome and tall. *This must be the one God has chosen,* Samuel said to himself.

~ BEDTIME BLESSING ~

God knows everything about you.

But God said Eliab wasn't the one! "I look at the heart," God told Samuel, "not at what someone looks like on the outside."

One by one, six other sons of Jesse stood before Samuel. But none of them was the one God had chosen.

"Do you have any other sons?" Samuel asked Jesse.

"Just one," Jesse said. "David. He is the youngest. He is out in the fields caring for the sheep."

"Call him," Samuel said. "We can't have dinner until he comes."

When David came in from the fields, God told Samuel, "This is the one I have chosen."

Samuel poured oil over David's head as a sign that God had chosen him. David, the shepherd boy who loved God with all his heart and wanted to do what God said, would be Israel's next king.

☙ SLEEPY-TIME PRAYER ❧

Dear God, I'm glad You know everything about me and care about my heart. I want to love You with all my heart! Good night, God! Amen.

The Small and the Tall

1 Samuel 17

GOD'S WORDS TO DREAM ON

Our God is a God who saves!
—Psalm 68:20 NLT

While David waited for the right time to be king, he kept on caring for his father's sheep. Some of David's brothers joined the army to fight against the Philistines. Then Jesse sent David to check on his brothers and bring them food.

When David got to the army camp, he put down the bundles of food and went to find his brothers. He found them just as the armies were lining up for battle. One Philistine soldier was over nine feet tall! His name was Goliath. David watched as Goliath stepped forward and started making fun of the Israelites, just as he had been doing every day for forty days.

"Come on! Send someone out to fight me!" Goliath yelled. "I dare you!" He waved his giant-sized spear and stomped his giant-sized feet. But King Saul and all of Israel's soldiers were afraid of him. No one would fight Goliath.

No one except David.

"I will fight Goliath," he told King Saul.

"How can you fight Goliath?" the king said. "You're just a boy!"

"God will help me," David said.

"Put on my helmet and my armor then," said King Saul.

David tried on the king's helmet and armor. "I can't wear this," he said. "It is too heavy. I'm not used to it." David took five smooth stones from a stream and put them in his shepherd's bag. Then he marched out to face Goliath.

The giant laughed at David. "Who do you think you are?" he yelled. "You can't hurt me!"

David answered, "You have a sword, a spear, and a javelin, but I come to you in the name of the Lord! He is the One you are fighting. Today everyone will see that there is a God in Israel and that He is the One who saves!" David ran toward the giant and threw a stone at Goliath with his slingshot.

Thud! The stone hit Goliath in the head. He fell on his face on the ground. The battle was over, and the Philistines ran away.

Dear God, I know that even when I have a giant-sized problem, You will help me. Thank You for being the One who saves us! Good night, God! Amen.

✺ BEDTIME BLESSING ✺
God will fight for you.

What Solomon Wanted

1 Kings 2–3; 10

⊷ GOD'S WORDS TO DREAM ON ⊷

Wisdom begins with respect for
the Lord. —Psalm 111:10 ICB

King David had many children, but God chose David's son Solomon to be the next king.

"Stay strong, Solomon," King David told his son. "Always do what God says is right."

When the time came for him to be king, Solomon wondered if he could be a good king like his father. Solomon loved God and tried to do what God says is right, but being king was such a big job!

One night after Solomon had been worshipping God, God came to Solomon in a dream. "Ask Me for whatever you want," God said. "What would you like for Me to give you?"

That was a big question! What would Solomon's answer be? Solomon could ask God for *anything*!

"You were so good to my father, David," Solomon said to God. "And now You have made me king in his place, even though I'm young. I want to be a

good king for Your people. So I will ask for that. Give me wisdom to know how to be a good king, to know right from wrong."

Solomon's request pleased God. "You have not asked for riches or honor or a long life for yourself," God said. "You haven't asked for harm to come upon your enemies. So I will give you what you asked for—wisdom to know what is right. And I will also give you what you did not ask for—riches and honor. You will be greater than any other king as long as you live. And if you obey Me and follow My laws like your father David did, I will give you long life too."

Solomon awoke from his dream. He felt glad because God had answered his prayer. He worshipped God and fixed a big feast for all his friends.

BEDTIME BLESSING
God's Word will give you wisdom.

God did give Solomon riches and honor and great wisdom. Solomon knew what was right and what was wrong. Rulers from other countries came to visit Solomon to hear what he had to say. When people came to him with a problem, he made good decisions for them, and everyone knew his wisdom came from God.

❧ SLEEPY-TIME PRAYER ❧

Dear God, I want to be wise and to understand what is right and what is wrong. I'm glad Your words in the Bible will teach me to be wise. Good night, God! Amen.

Birds and Bread

1 Kings 17

I trust in God. I will not be afraid. —Psalm 56:11 ICB

Even though King Solomon had great wisdom, he didn't always use it. He and the kings who came after him chose to do things God said not to do, and the people began to forget about God.

But God loved His people. He sent them prophets with messages to remind them to follow Him. One of those prophets was Elijah.

Elijah went to see King Ahab, a very bad king. "There won't be any rain until I say so," Elijah told the king. The message made King Ahab angry. To keep Elijah safe from angry King Ahab, God told Elijah, "Go to the brook called Cherith and stay there. I have told the ravens to bring you food each day."

Elijah obeyed God. He camped out near the brook, where King Ahab couldn't find him. Each morning and each evening, the ravens flew to Elijah's campsite with meat and bread in their beaks for him to eat!

But after a while, the brook dried up because there was no rain. Then God told Elijah, "Go to the town of Zarephath. A woman there will feed you now." At the gate of the town, Elijah saw a woman gathering sticks to build a cooking fire. He asked her to give him some bread.

"I have only a little flour and oil left to bake bread for my son and me," she said. "And I don't know what we will eat after that."

"Don't be afraid," Elijah said. "Use the last of your oil and flour to bake bread for me. Then bake bread for yourself and your son. God says He will give you flour and oil every day until it rains again!"

The woman shook the last of her flour out of her flour jar. She poured the last of her oil out of her jug of oil. She mixed the flour and oil together and baked bread for Elijah. Then she looked in the flour jar again—and she saw flour in the jar! She looked in the jug of oil again—and she saw oil in the jug! Just as God had promised!

That day, and every day afterward until it rained again, the woman and her son had flour and oil for baking bread, and they shared it with Elijah.

∾ SLEEPY-TIME PRAYER ∾

Dear God, just as You took care of people in the Bible, I know You take care of me. I don't need to be afraid. Good night, God! Amen.

∾ BEDTIME BLESSING ∾
God takes care of you.

Jonah Runs Away

The Book of Jonah

⊰ GOD'S WORDS TO DREAM ON ⊱

God, the people should praise you. All people should praise you. —Psalm 67:3 ICB

God told Jonah, "Go to Nineveh and preach to the people there."

Go to Nineveh? That wicked city? Jonah didn't want to go *there*. The people of Nineveh didn't worship God, and Jonah didn't want God to show kindness to *them*. So Jonah got on a ship ready to sail far away from Nineveh. "I'm running away from God," he told the sailors.

But God always knows where we are! He sent a strong storm to the sea. The wind and waves battered the ship until it almost broke apart. The sailors cried out in fear and tried hard to save the ship. "Make the ship lighter!" they shouted. "Throw the cargo overboard!"

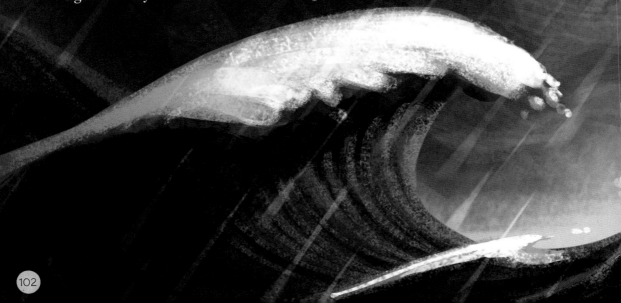

All this time, Jonah was sound asleep.

"Get up!" the ship's captain yelled to Jonah. "How can you sleep? Ask your God to help us!"

"Maybe Jonah is the problem," the sailors said. "He told us he was running away from God." The sailors found Jonah and asked him, "Where are you from? What kind of work do you do?"

"I am a Hebrew," Jonah said, "and I worship God, who made the sea and the land."

The sea was getting rougher, crashing and splashing against the ship. "What have you done?" the sailors asked Jonah. "What can we do to make the sea calm again?"

Well, the sailors didn't want to do *that*! They kept trying to row the ship to shore. But finally, they did what Jonah said. And the sea grew calm right away.

Jonah drifted down, down, down into the sea, but God sent a big fish to swallow Jonah so he wouldn't drown. For three days, Jonah lay in the smelly belly of that big fish. "Thank You for saving me, God," he prayed. Then God told the fish to let Jonah out. The big fish got a tummy ache and threw up Jonah onto dry ground.

"Go to Nineveh," God told Jonah again.

This time Jonah obeyed. He went to Nineveh and gave the people God's warning. The people believed God and decided to start doing right, which pleased God very much. "I care about all those people," God told Jonah. "They are important to Me."

BEDTIME BLESSING

Everyone matters to God—including you!

❧ SLEEPY-TIME PRAYER ❧

Dear God, I'm glad You care about every person! Help me to care about everyone too. Help me to tell people how good You are! Good night, God! Amen.

Daniel and the Hungry Lions

Daniel 6

Hear my prayer, O LORD. —Psalm 143:1

The Israelites and their kings often forgot about God and disobeyed Him. God had told them many times, "If you keep forgetting Me and don't obey My laws, someday you will have to leave the Promised Land." That sad time came when Daniel was a young man. Even some Israelites who *did* love God were captured and taken to other lands. Daniel and his friends were some of those people.

Daniel treated everyone well. He was wise and used his wisdom to help the king. And three times every day, Daniel knelt down beside his open window and prayed to God.

The king's other helpers were jealous of Daniel. They tried to find a way to make him lose his job. "But Daniel doesn't do anything wrong!" they said.

Then they had an idea, and they went to see the king. "O king, you are so great!" they said. "You should make a rule that everyone must pray only to you for thirty days. And if anyone doesn't pray only to you, throw him into the lions' den to be eaten by the lions!"

Now, the king should have known that this was a *bad* idea. He should have thought about his friend Daniel, who always prayed to God. But he didn't. The king made a law that everyone in the kingdom must pray only to him for thirty days or be thrown into a den of hungry lions.

When Daniel heard about the new law, he didn't worry. At his open window, he still prayed to God just as he always had. The king's other helpers spied on Daniel. They saw him praying to God, and they ran to tell the king.

The king felt ashamed, but the law couldn't be changed. "May your God keep you safe!" the king said. Then Daniel was flung into the den of hungry lions. The king went back to his palace, but he couldn't sleep.

In the morning, the king ran to the lions' den. "Daniel!" he cried. "Has your God kept you safe?" Oh, how the king hoped he would hear Daniel's voice!

"Yes, King!" Daniel called to him. "My God sent an angel to close the mouths of all the hungry lions." Daniel came out of the lions' den, and the king could see that Daniel hadn't been hurt at all.

"Daniel's God is the living God!" the king said. "And all the people in my kingdom should worship Him forever!"

SLEEPY-TIME PRAYER

Dear God, tonight I'm
praying to You, just as
Daniel prayed to You.
Thank You for Your love
and care for me. I love You,
God. Good night! Amen.

BEDTIME BLESSING

You can pray to God
no matter what.

New Walls and a Long Wait

Nehemiah 1–4; 6; 8

✧ GOD'S WORDS TO DREAM ON ✧

For to us a child is born, to us a
son is given. —Isaiah 9:6

God had promised He would one day bring His people back to their land. And He did! After seventy years, the people returned to Jerusalem. They built a new temple for God.

But the city walls were broken down, and the city gates had been burned. And they stayed that way for a long time.

When he heard about it, Nehemiah felt very sad, and he wanted to help. Nehemiah worked for the king of Persia. He prayed to God, and then he went to speak to the king.

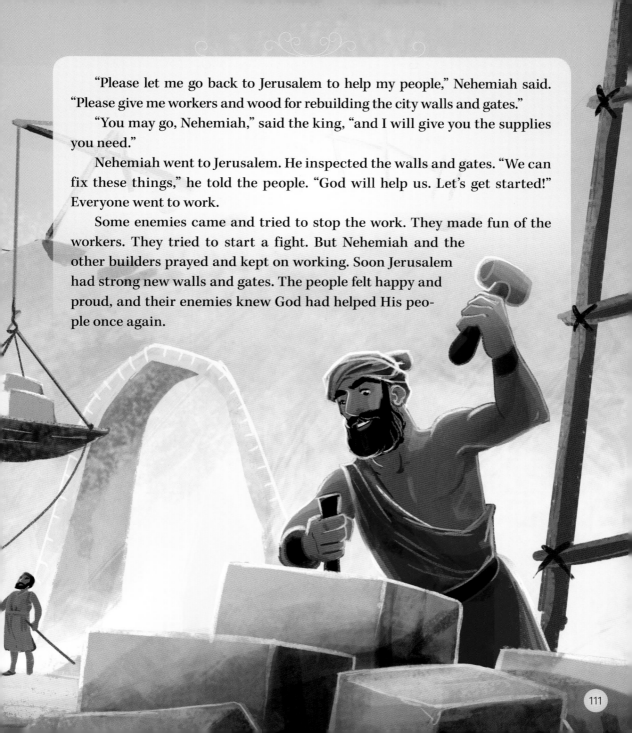

"Please let me go back to Jerusalem to help my people," Nehemiah said. "Please give me workers and wood for rebuilding the city walls and gates."

"You may go, Nehemiah," said the king, "and I will give you the supplies you need."

Nehemiah went to Jerusalem. He inspected the walls and gates. "We can fix these things," he told the people. "God will help us. Let's get started!" Everyone went to work.

Some enemies came and tried to stop the work. They made fun of the workers. They tried to start a fight. But Nehemiah and the other builders prayed and kept on working. Soon Jerusalem had strong new walls and gates. The people felt happy and proud, and their enemies knew God had helped His people once again.

Ezra the priest read the book of God's laws to all the men, women, and children who were old enough to understand. The people listened carefully. They cried because they were so happy to hear God's words again. Ezra praised God, and the people lifted their hands and said, "Amen! Amen!"

"Don't cry or be sad today," Nehemiah and Ezra told the people. "Today is a happy, good day and a time for celebrating! The joy of the Lord is your strength!" So the people went back to their homes, rejoicing.

God had kept His promises. Abraham's family had become a great nation and lived in the Promised Land. And now the people were back in their land once again.

But God also had promised to send Someone to the world to make things right again. He would keep that promise too, at just the right time, even if it meant a long wait.

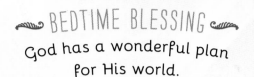

BEDTIME BLESSING

God has a wonderful plan for His world.

SLEEPY-TIME PRAYER

Dear God, thank You for all Your words and promises. I'm happy because You have a good plan for Your world and for me. Good night, God! Amen.

New Testament Stories

"You can be sure that
I will be with you always."
—Matthew 28:20 ICB

One Silent Night

Luke 1–2

When the right time came, God sent
his Son. —Galatians 4:4 ICB

Do you remember reading about Adam and Eve? They had to leave the garden of Eden, but God said that someday Someone would come to make things right again. Later on, God made that same promise to His people, the Israelites, through His messengers the prophets.

But no one guessed that the One to come would be God Himself—*Immanuel*, which means "God with us."

God sent the angel Gabriel to the town of Nazareth to visit Mary, a young woman engaged to marry a man named Joseph. Mary was surprised to see an angel!

"Don't be afraid, Mary!" the angel said kindly. "God is pleased with you. You are going to have a baby! He will be God's own Son, and you will name Him Jesus. He will rule God's people forever."

Mary listened carefully to what the angel said. "How will I have a baby," she asked, "since I'm not married?"

"The power of God will make it happen," Gabriel said.

"I am God's servant," Mary answered. "Let everything happen as you have told me."

The angel left, and Mary went to visit her relative Elizabeth. Mary sang a joyful song: "My soul praises the Lord; my heart is happy because God is my Savior. . . . God has done what he promised to our ancestors, to Abraham and to his children forever" (Luke 1:46–47, 55 ICB).

Later on, the Roman emperor made a new law: everyone in the empire must register and be counted in their family towns. Joseph traveled back to Bethlehem, his family town, to be counted along with Mary.

While they were there, the time came for Mary's baby to be born. But Bethlehem was full of travelers, with no room for Mary and Joseph at the inn. They found a quiet place to rest among the animals nearby.

That night Jesus was born! He was God, *and* He was human. He was Immanuel, God with us. Just as God had promised!

Mary wrapped the baby in strips of cloth and held Him lovingly. And when He fell asleep, the animals' hay-filled feeding trough served as His bed. Mary gently laid Him there to dream in the silent night.

SLEEPY-TIME PRAYER

Dear God, thank You for sending Your Son, Jesus, to earth! What a special baby! Good night, God! Amen.

BEDTIME BLESSING

God sent Jesus to
the world—and to you.

Good News for All People

Matthew 2; Luke 2

I bring you good news of
great joy. —Luke 2:10

On the night Jesus was born, sleepy shepherds watched over their sheep near Bethlehem. Suddenly, an angel came to talk to them, and the dark night sky turned bright with light. What could be happening?

"Don't be afraid!" the angel said. "I have good news!"

Good news for shepherds? Why would God have good news for them? Shepherds got dirty and smelly and couldn't take many baths. People made fun of them.

120

"I have good news of great joy for *all* people!" the angel said. "Today in Bethlehem a baby has been born. He is the Savior, the One God promised to send! Go to see Him! You will find Him wrapped in cloths and lying in a manger."

Then the sky filled with angels—all the angels of heaven—praising God for sending Jesus. "Glory to God!" they said. "Peace to people on earth!" What a beautiful sound those shepherds must have heard!

The angels left, and the sky was quiet. "Let's go find the baby!" the shepherds said. They hurried into Bethlehem and searched until they found Mary and Joseph and the baby, resting among the animals.

"It's Him!" the shepherds said. "He is wrapped in cloths and lying in a manger, just as the angel said. This baby is the Savior, the One God promised to send!"

Everyone who heard the shepherds' good news couldn't stop talking about it. But Mary quietly thought about every word.

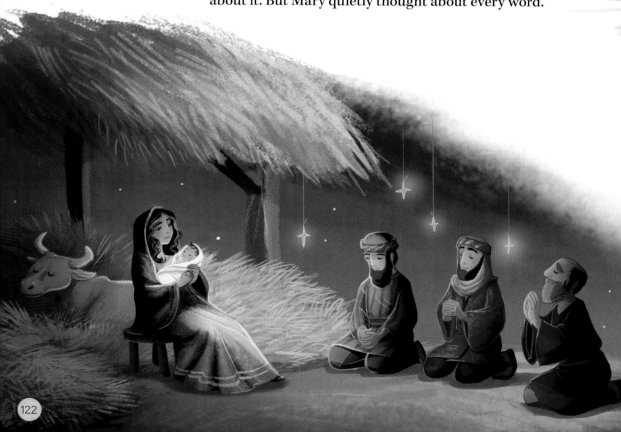

The shepherds went back to their sheep, thanking God for everything they had seen and heard. And far away, wise men from the East noticed a new star in the sky. "Look!" they said. "It's the star of the newborn King!" They wanted to see the baby too. So they saddled up their camels and set out on a long journey, following the star.

SLEEPY-TIME PRAYER

Dear God, thank You that the good news
about Jesus is for all people, including
me. I love You, God. Good night! Amen.

Taller, Stronger, Wiser

Luke 2

⋙ GOD'S WORDS TO DREAM ON ⋘

The child grew and became strong,
filled with wisdom. —Luke 2:40

124

Mary and Joseph took good care of Jesus, and of course God was watching over Him too. The little family settled back in Nazareth, where Jesus grew taller, stronger, and wiser every day. People enjoyed knowing Him, and God was pleased with Him.

When He was twelve, Jesus went with Mary and Joseph and others from Nazareth to Jerusalem, where the temple was. They went there to celebrate Passover, a time to remember how God had rescued His people from slavery in Egypt long ago.

When the week ended and everyone started walking home, Mary and Joseph didn't see Jesus, but they thought He was with their family and friends. But when they stopped for the night, they couldn't find Jesus anywhere! "Oh, Joseph, I'm so worried!" Mary might have said. Mary and Joseph turned around and hurried back to Jerusalem. They searched for Him all the next day. Where could He be?

Finally, they found Jesus in the temple, sitting with the men who taught people about God. He was listening to the teachers and asking them questions. The teachers asked Jesus questions too, and His answers amazed everyone.

"Jesus!" Mary said. "Why didn't You tell us You were staying in Jerusalem? We have been searching for You, and we have been so worried!"

"Why were you looking for Me, Mother?" Jesus asked. "Didn't you know I needed to be in My Father's house?" Mary and Joseph didn't understand this. But Jesus always obeyed Mary and Joseph, so He left the temple with them and went home to Nazareth.

Mary remembered and thought about all these things in her heart. And Jesus kept growing—stronger, taller, wiser, and pleasing to people and to God.

SLEEPY-TIME PRAYER

Dear God, thank You for helping Jesus grow up
tall, strong, and wise. Please help me grow up in
good ways too. Good night, God! Amen.

BEDTIME BLESSING

Jesus grew, and you
are growing too.

This Is My Son

Matthew 3

✦ GOD'S WORDS TO DREAM ON ✦

Call on the Lord from a pure
heart. —2 Timothy 2:22

Jesus grew from a baby to a boy to a man. When He was thirty years old, He began to preach and teach and do the work God had sent Him to do.

First, though, God wanted people to get ready to listen to Jesus. So God sent John the Baptist, Jesus' cousin, with a message for everyone to hear: "Get ready! The kingdom of God is near! Prepare the way of the Lord!"

John lived in the desert. He wore clothes made of camel hair, with a leather belt around his waist. He ate locusts and wild honey. People in Jerusalem and all around wanted to see and hear him. "You need to repent," John told them. "Stop doing wrong things, and start doing right things." John baptized the people who heard his words and did what he said.

Some leaders came to listen to John, but they didn't want to be baptized. They didn't think they did anything wrong. They didn't know that God cared more about their hearts than about how well they kept His laws. God wanted them to obey because they loved Him.

"Someone much more important than me is coming," John told them. "Someone powerful and mighty! He can change your hearts and help you love and obey God." John was talking about Jesus.

Then Jesus came out to the Jordan River to be baptized. But Jesus had never done anything wrong! "I need to be baptized by *You*," John told Jesus. "Why are You coming here to me?"

"This is the right thing to do," Jesus said, "and God wants Me to do it."

So John baptized Jesus. When Jesus stood up in the water, the sky opened above Him, and God's Spirit came down in the form of a dove and rested on Jesus. Then a voice from heaven—God's voice—said, "This is My Son, and I am very pleased with Him."

❦ SLEEPY-TIME PRAYER ❧

Dear God, thank You for sending Your
Son, Jesus. Thank You for caring about
my heart! Good night, God! Amen.

131

So Many Fish!

Matthew 4; Mark 1; Luke 5

❧ GOD'S WORDS TO DREAM ON ❧

Jesus said, "Come follow
me." —Matthew 4:19 ICB

People loved to hear Jesus teach about God. One day, by the Sea of Galilee, Jesus got into a fishing boat and asked the fisherman to row the boat out on the lake a short distance. Then Jesus taught the crowd from the boat.

When He had finished teaching, Jesus told the fisherman, Simon Peter, "Take the boat far out on the lake and put your nets in for a catch."

"I fished all night and caught nothing," Peter said. "I don't think there are any fish out there right now. But because You are telling me to do it, I will."

So Peter and his brother, Andrew, rowed the boat far out on the lake, with Jesus in the boat. They threw their fishing nets into the water, and down, down, down went the nets. Then Peter and Andrew waited—but not for long! Suddenly, the nets started breaking because they were so full of fish!

"Come and help us!" Peter and Andrew yelled to their friends James and John, in another boat. The fishermen pulled up the nets and filled both boats with fish—so many fish in each boat that the boats began to sink!

The fish hadn't been there earlier—Peter and Andrew and James and John were sure of it. So where had they all come from?

Peter knew that Jesus had done it. He knelt down in front of Jesus. "You're so strong and good," Peter said, "and I'm so weak and do many wrong things. You should go away from me now."

But Jesus just smiled at Peter. "Don't be afraid," Jesus said. "From now on, come and follow Me, and start fishing for people!" Jesus meant that instead of catching fish with nets, they would start catching people with God's love.

Peter and Andrew and James and John rowed their boats back to shore. And from then on, they followed Jesus wherever He went.

∾ SLEEPY-TIME PRAYER ∾

Dear God, I want to follow Jesus! Please help me be good at fishing for people—help me tell others all about Jesus' love. Good night, God! Amen.

Down Through the Roof

Mark 2; Luke 5

⤜⛈ GOD'S WORDS TO DREAM ON ⛈⤛

Everyone who believes in Jesus will
be forgiven. —Acts 10:43 ICB

"We're almost there!" said four friends carrying a man on a mat. "We're almost at the house where Jesus is!"

The man on the mat was paralyzed—he couldn't move. He and his friends wanted Jesus to make him well. But when they got to the house where Jesus was, there were so many people! The four friends and the man on the mat couldn't even see the door. What would they do?

Carefully, they carried the man on his mat up to the roof, and then they started making a hole in the roof! Inside the house, everyone looked *up* just in time to see the man on his mat coming down through the roof—right in front of Jesus!

"I forgive all the wrong things you have done," Jesus told the man.

Some leaders in the house thought, *Only God can forgive sins. Who does Jesus think He is?*

"Is it easier to forgive sins or to heal?" Jesus asked. "But

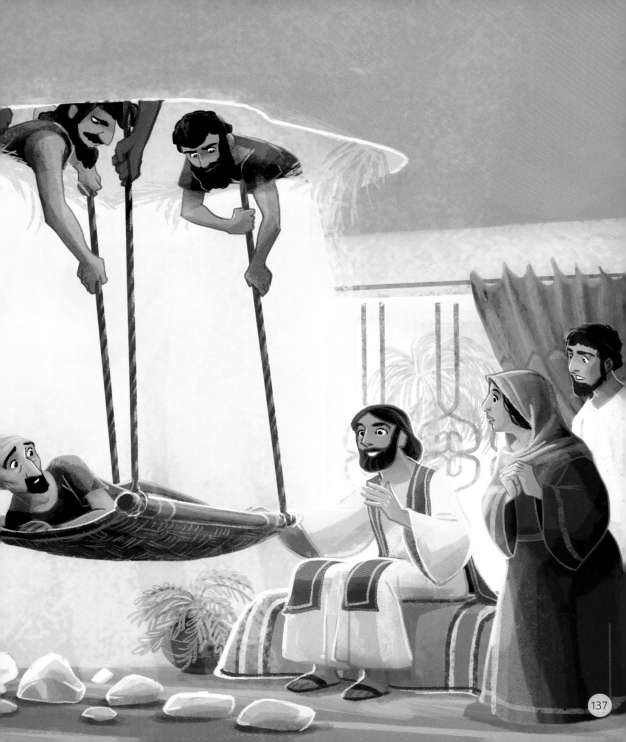

to prove that I have authority to forgive sins—" He turned to the man on the mat and said, "Get up, pick up your mat, and go home."

What would happen? No one said a word. Then the man on the mat stood up! He rolled up his mat and walked out the door, heading home, just as Jesus had told him to do.

All the people started praising God. "We have never seen anything like this before!" they said.

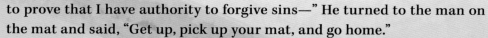

Dear God, I'm glad the man on the mat had friends who cared about him. Thank You for people who help me know Jesus. I'm glad You sent Jesus to help and forgive. Good night, God! Amen.

❧ BEDTIME BLESSING ❧
Jesus forgives you.

Jesus Chooses Twelve

Matthew 10; Mark 3; Luke 6

❧ GOD'S WORDS TO DREAM ON ☙

Pray about everything. —Philippians 4:6 NLT

At the end of a busy day, as it was getting dark, Jesus went outside for a walk. He walked until He came near a mountain, and He began to climb the mountain. After a while, He stopped climbing and found a comfortable place to rest. Maybe He looked up at the night sky, filled with twinkling stars. Then Jesus began praying to His Father, God.

Jesus often got alone like this to pray. But this time He prayed to God all night long. Sometimes He talked, and sometimes He listened. He had an important decision to make. He needed to choose twelve special helpers from among His disciples. Who should they be?

When morning came, Jesus finished praying. He had made His decision. He called the disciples together and told them the names of the twelve He had chosen.

Jesus chose:
Simon (Jesus called him Peter),
Andrew (Peter's brother),
James and John (Jesus nicknamed these brothers the Sons of Thunder),
Philip, Bartholomew, Matthew, and Thomas,
James the son of Alpheus,
another Simon,
Thaddeus,
and Judas.

These twelve disciples would travel everywhere with Jesus and be His good friends—all except one, Judas (but that was part of God's plan). They would learn from Jesus. They would listen to everything He said and see everything He did. Jesus also sent out these disciples to preach and teach, to practice for the work they would do later on when Jesus wasn't with them anymore.

～ BEDTIME BLESSING ～
You can pray to God.

Jesus' prayer that night was important! Soon the helpers Jesus chose would be known as His apostles and would start sharing the good news about Jesus for everyone to hear!

SLEEPY-TIME PRAYER

Dear God, thank You for Jesus' helpers and the work Jesus gave them to do. Please help me to always pray to You like Jesus did. Good night, God! Amen.

Wind and Sea Obey Him

Matthew 8; Mark 4; Luke 8

❧ GOD'S WORDS TO DREAM ON ❧

God's power is very great for us
who believe. —Ephesians 1:19 ICB

Wherever He went, Jesus taught about God and how God wants us to live. "What a good teacher Jesus is!" said the people who heard Him teach. "We learn so much about God. Jesus seems to really know what He is talking about."

And, of course, He really did.

One day, after teaching for a long time, Jesus got into a boat on the Sea of Galilee with His twelve disciples. "Let's go across to the other side," He said.

Jesus felt tired. He lay down on a cushion at the back of the boat, and soon He was fast asleep.

The sea got stormy. Gusts of wind blew against the boat—*whoo, whoo, whoosh!* The boat rocked on its side as the wind got stronger. Big waves of water knocked against the boat too.

Jesus didn't wake up.

The wind blew harder, and the waves got bigger. The disciples tried to keep the boat headed in the right direction. But the boat bobbed around on the sea like a bouncing ball.

"Look out!" the disciples yelled. Waves started crashing into the boat and filling it with water.

Jesus didn't wake up.

"What should we do?" the disciples yelled. "We're all going to drown!"

Finally, the disciples went to the back of the boat where Jesus was still sleeping. "Jesus! Jesus! Wake up!" they shouted. "Don't You care about the trouble we're having? Save us!"

Jesus got up. He wasn't upset or worried. "Hush!" He said to the wildly blowing wind and the surging sea. "Peace. Be still."

Suddenly, everything grew quiet. No more wind. No more waves.

"Why were you afraid?" Jesus asked His friends. "Where is your faith?"

Now the disciples felt more amazed by Jesus than they ever had before. Even the wind and the sea obeyed Him!

SLEEPY-TIME PRAYER

Dear God, when I have a problem, I will ask Jesus to help me. Thank You for Jesus and His mighty power. He helps me feel safe. Good night, God! Amen.

Jesus the Healer

Matthew 9; Mark 5; Luke 8

❧ GOD'S WORDS TO DREAM ON ❧

"I am the Lord who heals you."
—Exodus 15:26 ICB

Jesus often healed people who were sick. Sometimes He touched them to make them well. Other times He just spoke. And once, someone reached out to touch *Him*.

People from near and far filled the street, hoping to see Jesus. A woman in the crowd had been sick a long time. No doctors had been able to help her. But maybe Jesus would! She really wanted Him to, and she believed He could.

The woman moved closer to Jesus in the crowd until she was right behind Him. *If I just touch the edge of His clothing*, she said to herself, *He will make me well.* She reached out and touched the edge of His cloak. And right away, she felt well!

"Who touched Me?" Jesus said.

All around Him, people said, "Not me," "Not me," and "It wasn't me."

"There are so many people on the street with us," Jesus' friend Peter said. "Everyone wants to get close to You. Someone must have just bumped into You."

"No," Jesus said. "Someone touched Me on purpose, and I felt power go out of Me." He turned and saw the woman who had been healed.

Oh dear! Was Jesus angry with her? The woman bowed in front of Jesus. "I'm the one, sir," she said. "I have been sick for many years. No doctors could help me. I wanted to be well, and I believed You could heal me. I thought that if I just touched the edge of Your cloak, I would be healed. And as soon as I touched You, I was well!"

Jesus smiled as He spoke kindly to the woman. "Your faith in Me has healed you," He said. "Don't be afraid, and go in peace."

~SLEEPY-TIME PRAYER~

Dear God, thank You for sending Jesus the healer. Thank You for making me well when I get sick! Good night, God! Amen.

BEDTIME BLESSING

Jesus has power to
make you well.

151

Feeding a Crowd

Matthew 14; Mark 6; Luke 9; John 6

He cares for you. —1 Peter 5:7

On a hillside far from towns and villages, Jesus had been teaching thousands of people all day. Now it was getting late, and the people in the crowd were getting hungry. Their tummies made *rumble-grumble* noises.

Jesus wanted the people to have something to eat before they started their long walk home. "You can feed them," He told His disciples.

"How can we do that?" they asked. "We don't have enough money to buy food for all these people! And besides, there's no place nearby to buy anything."

But Jesus knew exactly what He was going to do.

"Does anyone in the crowd have any food?" He asked them. "Go find out."

Andrew brought a boy and his small lunch to Jesus—five round loaves of barley bread and two dried fish. "But this is not enough for so many people!" Andrew said.

"Tell the people to sit down in groups of fifty or so," Jesus answered.

In all the grassy places on the hillside, the people sat in groups and waited.

Jesus looked up to heaven and thanked God for the bread and fish. Then He broke the loaves into pieces and gave bread to the disciples to give to every group. He broke the fish into pieces too and gave fish to the disciples to give to every group.

Everyone got plenty of bread and fish. The five loaves of bread and two small fish didn't run out! All the men, women, and children ate until they were full!

After the meal, Jesus told His disciples, "Now go and gather up the leftovers." They brought back twelve baskets full of bread and fish!

The people saw that Jesus had turned just a little food into more than enough for everyone in the crowd. "Surely He is the One we have been waiting for!" they said.

~ BEDTIME BLESSING ~

Jesus provides everything you need.

SLEEPY-TIME PRAYER

Dear God, thank You for taking care of me. Thank You for good food to eat when I'm hungry. Thank You for Jesus! Good night, God! Amen.

Who's the Greatest?

Matthew 18; Mark 9; Luke 9; John 13

❧ GOD'S WORDS TO DREAM ON ☙

Serve each other with love.
—Galatians 5:13 ICB

Jesus walked along the dusty road to Capernaum with His disciples. After a while, the disciples started arguing among themselves about who was the greatest in the kingdom of heaven.

Maybe they talked about which one of them knew the most about God, or who spoke the best or healed the most people when Jesus sent them out to preach. Maybe they talked about who prayed the best prayers or gave the most money at the temple.

Maybe they thought whoever was the greatest would get a big reward.

When they got to the house in Capernaum where they would stay, even though He already knew, Jesus asked, "What were you talking about on the way here?"

They didn't want to tell Him. Maybe they felt embarrassed about it. *What will Jesus think?* they might have wondered.

Jesus called a child to come and stand among the disciples. "Those who are humble, like this child, are the greatest," He said. "Children know they must depend on someone else."

Jesus had another example for His friends. "Those who don't try to be important are the greatest," He said. "They put others first. They help and serve other people."

Later on, at a special dinner, Jesus showed His friends more about how to be humble. Jesus served His friends by washing their feet. He took off their sandals and did the work a servant would do. He had a big bowl of water for washing off the dust from the street and a big towel wrapped around His waist for drying.

"Do you understand why I washed your feet?" Jesus asked His friends when He was done. "I have given you an example. I am your teacher and your Lord. So if I have served you by washing your feet, you also should serve each other."

⌘ BEDTIME BLESSING ⌘
You can humbly serve other people.

⌘ SLEEPY-TIME PRAYER ⌘
Dear God, every day, show me how I can help and serve other people. I want to serve others like Jesus did. Good night, God! Amen.

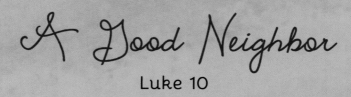

A Good Neighbor

Luke 10

❧ GOD'S WORDS TO DREAM ON ❧

"Love your neighbor as you love yourself." —Leviticus 19:18 ICB

A scribe (a man who knew a lot about God's laws) asked Jesus, "What must I do to live forever?"

"You know the law," Jesus answered. "What does it say?"

"Love the Lord your God with all

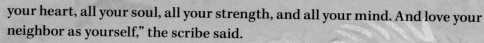

your heart, all your soul, all your strength, and all your mind. And love your neighbor as yourself," the scribe said.

"That is right," Jesus said. "Do those things."

"Well . . ." the scribe said, "just who *is* my neighbor?" He didn't really want to love *everyone*.

Then Jesus told this story:

Robbers hurt a man traveling on the road to Jericho. They beat him up and took his money and left him lying in the road, badly hurt.

After a while, a priest came walking down the road. He saw the hurt man lying there, but he didn't stop to help. In fact, he passed by on the other side of the road.

A little while later, a temple worker came walking down the road. He saw the hurt man lying there, but he didn't stop to help either. In fact, he passed by on the other side of the road too.

Then a Samaritan came down the road, riding on a donkey. When the Samaritan saw the hurt man lying in the road, he stopped right away. He felt sorry for the man. He bandaged up the hurt man's wounds, put him on the donkey he had been riding, and took him to an inn. He stayed with the hurt man at

BEDTIME BLESSING

You can be a good neighbor.

162

the inn and took good care of him. Then he gave the innkeeper money for taking care of the hurt man until he was well.

After Jesus told this story, He asked, "Which of the three men was a neighbor to the hurt man—the priest, the temple worker, or the Samaritan?"

The scribe's question—who is my neighbor?—was the wrong question! The right question was, how can I be a good neighbor?

"The Samaritan was the good neighbor," the scribe answered. "He cared about the hurt man and helped him. He showed mercy."

"Yes," said Jesus. "Now you go and do the same."

⟨∾ SLEEPY-TIME PRAYER ∾⟩

Dear God, I want to be a good neighbor and
love other people. I want to be caring and kind.
Please help me. Good night, God! Amen.

The Most Important Thing

Luke 10

How sweet are your words. —Psalm 119:103

When Jesus and His disciples came to the village of Bethany and needed a place to stay, Martha invited them to stay at the home she shared with her sister, Mary, and her brother, Lazarus. And now Jesus and His disciples had arrived! Jesus sat in the living room, talking and teaching.

Martha wanted to fix Jesus a big, delicious dinner. *Hurry, hurry, hurry!* Everything needed to be just right!

Martha mixed and kneaded dough for baking bread. She gathered the meat and vegetables she would serve. She set out her cooking pots and started a fire in the oven. She washed and dried plates and platters and drinking cups and put them on the table.

Hurry, hurry, hurry!

Martha seasoned the meat. She washed and chopped the vegetables.

Hurry, hurry, hurry! Whew, this big dinner was lots of work! Too much work for just one person. Martha stopped chopping vegetables. *Where is my sister?* she wondered. *Why isn't she helping me?*

Martha wiped her hands on her apron and walked into the living room. She found Mary sitting on the floor, listening to Jesus as He taught.

Hmmph, thought Martha. *Maybe I'd like to be listening to Jesus too. But I don't have time. I'm busy getting dinner ready. Hurry, hurry, hurry! There's SO much work to do.* "Jesus, don't You think this is unfair?" Martha complained. "I'm doing all the work in the kitchen while Mary is out here listening to You! Tell Mary to come and help me!"

∽ BEDTIME BLESSING ∽

You can choose
to listen to Jesus.

"Martha, Martha," Jesus said. "You are worried and upset about so many things, aren't you? But only one thing is important—listening to Me. Your sister, Mary, has chosen the best thing. It won't be taken away from her."

We don't know what happened next, but maybe Martha decided to sit down for a while and listen to Jesus too!

⌁ SLEEPY-TIME PRAYER ⌁

Dear God, I want to always choose what is best and to hear Your wonderful words! I want to listen to Jesus. Good night, God! Amen.

A Father Forgives

Luke 15

God is love. —1 John 4:8

Jesus told a story to show what God's love is like:

A father had two sons. The older son, a hard worker on the family farm, always did what his father asked. But the younger son wanted a different life.

"Father," he said, "give me my share of the family money that is coming to me." The father knew this wouldn't make the son happy. But he didn't argue. He divided up the family property and gave his younger son the money.

In a few days, the younger son went off on a journey to a faraway land. He went to lots of parties and bought whatever he wanted. Soon he had spent all his money. Now how would he take care of himself?

He got a job feeding pigs.

"Here's your food, piggies," he said as he poured messy pig food into feeding troughs. He felt so hungry, though, that the messy pig food began to look good to him, and he thought about eating it himself.

Then he had an idea. "I'm a hired worker with nothing to eat," he said. "But my father gives plenty of food to his hired workers! I will go back to my father. I know I was wrong to leave home and waste all his money. I will ask him to let me be one of his hired workers." So he got up and began the journey home to his father.

Now, the son didn't know it, but his father watched for him every day. And when the son was still a long way off, his father saw him coming. Oh, how glad he was to see his son and how much he cared about all his son's troubles! The father ran to meet him and hugged and kissed him.

"Father, I have sinned," the son said. "Don't call me your son any longer. Just take me back as a hired worker."

But the father loved his son. He gave him new clothes and shoes and a beautiful ring. "We must celebrate now!" he called to everyone. "It's time for a party. My son is alive! He was lost, and now he is found!"

God loves and forgives us just like that father loved and forgave his son.

❧ SLEEPY-TIME PRAYER ❧

Dear God, I'm glad You always love me. I'm glad You're happy when lost people come back to Your love! Good night, God! Amen.

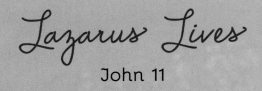

Lazarus Lives

John 11

"I am the resurrection and
the life." —John 11:25

When their brother, Lazarus, became sick, Mary and Martha sent a message to Jesus. They wanted Jesus to come to their home in the village of Bethany and make their brother well. But Jesus had another plan. He waited two days, and Lazarus died. Then Jesus went to Bethany.

When Martha heard that Jesus was coming, she went to meet Him. "Jesus, my brother would have lived if You had been here!" she said. She knew that Jesus loved Lazarus, and she didn't understand that Jesus had another plan.

"I am the resurrection and the life," Jesus told her. "Everyone who believes in Me will live, even if he dies. Do you believe this?"

"I believe You are God's Son, the One God sent to make things right," Martha told Him.

Then Mary went out to meet Jesus too. "Jesus, my brother would have lived if You had been here!" she said. She also knew that Jesus loved Lazarus, and she didn't understand that Jesus had another plan.

At the tomb where Lazarus was buried, many people were crying. Jesus cried too, because they were so sad. "Take away the stone," He said.

"We can't do that!" Martha said. "Lazarus has been buried for four days. There will be a bad smell."

"Didn't I tell you that if you believe, you will see the glory of God?" Jesus asked. So they took away the stone from the front of the tomb. Jesus prayed, "Father, may the people here believe that You sent Me." Then He said in a loud voice, "Lazarus, come out!"

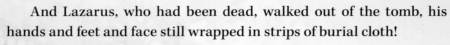

And Lazarus, who had been dead, walked out of the tomb, his hands and feet and face still wrapped in strips of burial cloth!

"Unbind him," Jesus said, "and let him go."

"If Jesus can raise someone from the dead, He *must* be the One God has sent," many of the people said, and they believed in Him.

~ BEDTIME BLESSING ~

Jesus gives life.

✦∞ SLEEPY-TIME PRAYER ∞✦

Dear God, I'm happy that Jesus made Lazarus
live again. I'm happy that Jesus gives life!
Good night, God! Amen.

Let the Children Come

Matthew 19; Mark 10; Luke 18

❧ GOD'S WORDS TO DREAM ON ❧

"Let the children come to me." —Mark 10:14

"We're going to see Jesus! We're going to see Jesus!" Boys and girls must have skipped, hopped, and jumped along the road. Their moms and dads, some carrying babies, walked beside them.

"When will we see Him?" the children asked.

"Soon," said the moms and dads. "Soon."

Then they saw Him, teaching people, with His disciples standing all around.

"Please, we want to see Jesus," the moms

and dads told the disciples. "We want Him to bless our children and pray for them. We've come a long way."

The disciples frowned. "Jesus can't take time for children," they said. "He's much too busy for that. Can't you see He's busy teaching?"

The boys and girls and moms and dads began to walk away, sad that they wouldn't get to see Jesus.

"Stop!" a voice said. It was Jesus' voice! "Come back, please."

The boys and girls ran back to Jesus. The moms and dads hurried back too, carrying the babies.

"Let the children come to me," Jesus told His disciples. "Never stop them or stand in their way. The kingdom of heaven belongs to such as these. In fact, if you don't enter the kingdom of heaven like a child, you'll never be able to go in."

Then Jesus took the children in His arms and blessed them and prayed for them. He held the babies and blessed and prayed for them too.

If you were one of those children, wouldn't you feel happy and safe and loved? Wouldn't you smile?

BEDTIME BLESSING

Jesus loves you so much!

SLEEPY-TIME PRAYER

Dear God, I'm glad Jesus loves me. I'm glad He loves every child in the whole world! I want children everywhere to know Jesus loves them. Good night, God! Amen.

Zacchaeus Meets Jesus

Luke 19

⚬⤳ GOD'S WORDS TO DREAM ON ⤲⚬

Lord, . . . you know all about
me. —Psalm 139:1 ICB

Zacchaeus saw people lining up on the streets of Jericho, hoping to see Jesus as He passed that way. Zacchaeus wanted to see Jesus too. But he was short, too short to see over the heads of the people in front of him. And no one would let him through to the front of the line. No one liked Zacchaeus because he was a tax collector who had gotten rich by cheating people.

"Oh, please let me through!" Zacchaeus said. But no one made room for him.

Then Zacchaeus had an idea. He ran to a nearby tree and climbed up in its branches. Now he could see everything—the street, all the people—and

Jesus—who came walking down the street toward the tree where Zacchaeus sat!

And then Jesus stopped right under the tree and looked up. "Zacchaeus, hurry and come down!" He said. "I need to stay at your house today!"

What? How did Jesus know his name? And why did Jesus want to stay at his house? Zacchaeus didn't know the answers, but he scurried down from the tree and joyfully took Jesus and His disciples home for dinner.

The people who saw this began to grumble. "Why is Jesus going to eat with a *tax collector*?" they said.

But even cheating tax collectors can change when they meet Jesus and listen to Him. And that's just what Zacchaeus did. "I'm going to give away half of everything I own," Zacchaeus told Jesus. "I will give it to the poor. And if I have cheated anyone, I'm going to pay him back four times as much!"

"I have come to seek and save the lost," Jesus said. "Salvation has come to this house today!"

~ BEDTIME BLESSING ~

Jesus knows you.

SLEEPY-TIME PRAYER

Dear God, I'm glad I have a friend like Jesus who knows everything about me and knows what I need. I'm glad Jesus cares about me! Good night, God! Amen.

Remember Me

Matthew 26; Mark 14; Luke 22

᪥ GOD'S WORDS TO DREAM ON ᪥

God sent his Son to die in
our place to take away our
sins. —1 John 4:10 ICB

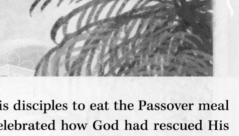

Jesus looked forward to being with His disciples to eat the Passover meal together. At Passover the Israelites celebrated how God had rescued His people from slavery and brought them out of Egypt. The roasted lamb and bread they ate reminded the people what God had done for them.

"Where should we go to prepare the Passover supper for You?" the disciples asked Jesus.

"Go into the city," Jesus said. "You'll meet a man carrying a water jar. Follow him to a house. The owner of the house will show you a large upstairs room. That's where we will eat. Get everything ready for our Passover supper there."

That evening Jesus and the disciples gathered around the table for the special feast. "I'm glad we could have this special celebration together tonight," Jesus said. "I won't eat it again until I eat it new with you in My Father's kingdom."

Jesus knew that soon He would finish the work God had given Him.

He would die on a cross for the sins of all people, so people could be free from sin on earth and live forever with God once again, the way God had always planned it. Jesus also knew that after He died, on the third day, He would rise again! He would see His friends and then go back to heaven. And someday Jesus' friends would be with Him in heaven too!

But right now Jesus wanted His friends to understand why He was going to die and to remember it always. So during the meal, Jesus picked up a loaf of bread and thanked God for it. Then He broke it into pieces and gave a piece to each of His friends. "This is My body, given for you," He said. "Whenever you eat the bread, do it to remember Me."

Next Jesus held up a cup. "Drink this," He said. "This is the new covenant—the new thing God is doing—in My blood. Every time you drink it, do it to remember Me."

~ BEDTIME BLESSING ~

Jesus wants us to remember Him.

When the meal was finished, Jesus and His friends sang a hymn—a song of praise to God—together.

⸻SLEEPY-TIME PRAYER⸻

Dear God, thank You for sending Jesus to us so we could live with You forever. Help me to remember Him always. Good night, God! Amen.

Sad Day, Glad Day

Matthew 27–28; Luke 23–24

✤ GOD'S WORDS TO DREAM ON ✤

God raised Jesus from the dead. —Acts 2:32 NLT

After their Passover meal, Jesus and His disciples went outside and walked to a garden. Jesus prayed there, and then soldiers came and arrested Him.

Even though Jesus had never done anything wrong—nothing at all—and even though He was the One God had sent, some leaders of God's people were jealous of Him. They wanted Jesus to die on a cross.

Jesus could have stopped all this from happening, but He didn't because it was part of God's plan. Still, the day Jesus died on the cross was a sad, dark day. The disciples didn't know what to do. A man named Joseph took Jesus' body down from the cross, laid it in a tomb, and rolled a big stone in front of the tomb.

But on the third day, Sunday, *everything* changed!

Some women got up before sunrise to go to Jesus' tomb. They took spices and ointments to place on Jesus' body. When they came to the tomb, the stone had been rolled away by an angel. They went inside, but the tomb was empty!

Suddenly, they saw two angels. "Why are you looking for Jesus here?" the angels asked. "He isn't here. He has risen, just as He said! Now go and

tell His disciples He is alive! Tell them to go to Galilee, where you will see Him."

What glad news! The women ran to tell the disciples what the angels had said. And on their way back into the city, they saw Jesus! They held His feet and worshipped Him, filled with joy.

"Don't be afraid," Jesus said. "Go and tell the disciples to go to Galilee, where they will see Me."

So the women hurried to find the disciples and tell them the glad news. They had seen Jesus—He was alive!

❧ SLEEPY-TIME PRAYER ☙

Dear God, thank You for the glad day when Jesus rose! Thank You that Jesus is alive! Good night, God! Amen.

He Will Come Again

Luke 24; John 21; Acts 1

❦ GOD'S WORDS TO DREAM ON ❧

We are eagerly waiting for him to
return. —Philippians 3:20 NLT

After Jesus rose, He spent time with His disciples, helping them understand what had happened. He met two of them as they walked along the road and reminded them what God's messengers, the prophets, had written.

"I am the One God sent," Jesus said. "Everything happened just as I told you. You saw all these things, so you are My witnesses. Now it's time for repentance and forgiveness to be preached to people all over the world."

Another day Peter and some of the other disciples went fishing, but they didn't catch anything. When they came back, they saw a man standing on the land, calling, "Friends, do you have any fish?"

"No," they said.

"Cast your net on the right side of the boat," the man said. So they did, and they caught 153 fish!

"It's Jesus!" Peter said. He wanted to see Jesus right away, so he dove into the water and swam toward the land.

Jesus had started a campfire and was warming bread and fish. He cooked some of the fish the disciples had caught too. Jesus and His friends ate breakfast together.

When the time came for Jesus to go back to heaven, He led His followers outside to a hill near a village called Bethany. "Go into all the world and make disciples," He said. "Tell people the good news about Me! Tell them they can believe in Me and be forgiven! But wait until I send you special power—the Holy Spirit of God."

As the disciples watched, Jesus went up into the clouds and disappeared. The disciples kept staring up at the sky even after they couldn't see Him anymore.

BEDTIME BLESSING

Jesus will come again.

Then two angels came and said, "Why are you looking up into heaven? Jesus has gone back to heaven now. Someday He will come again, in the same way you just saw Him go."

The disciples went back into the city, full of joy, and gathered in an upstairs room to praise God, and wait.

∽ SLEEPY-TIME PRAYER ∾

Dear God, thank You for everything Jesus did. Thank You that He will come back someday! Good night, God! Amen.

The Holy Spirit Comes

Acts 2

God gave us his Spirit. —1 John 4:13 ICB

After Jesus went back to heaven, the disciples often gathered upstairs in a house in Jerusalem. They remembered Jesus' instructions to wait for Him to send God's Holy Spirit.

One morning while they were all together in the house, they suddenly heard a loud noise from heaven, like a mighty wind. Then small tongues that looked like flames of fire came and rested on each one of them. They were all filled with the Holy Spirit and began to talk in different languages—languages they had never learned and didn't know how to speak!

Travelers from many countries had come to Jerusalem for the feast of Pentecost. They could hear the sound of all the disciples talking in different languages. What was going on? The travelers hurried to find out.

Surprise! Each person could hear Jesus' disciples praising God in his own language! "What does this mean?" the people wanted to know.

Peter answered the people's question. "Listen to me, all of you," he said. "The Holy Spirit has come today! God promised through the prophet Joel that the Holy Spirit would come, and now it has happened. And God also promised to send His Son, Jesus, to be the Savior!"

The people listened while Peter told them about Jesus. "Jesus died on the cross," he said, "but God raised Him from the dead! We saw Him alive again. Now He is back in heaven, and He has sent the Holy Spirit. Jesus is Lord!"

"What should we do?" the people asked Peter.

BEDTIME BLESSING

Jesus sent the Holy Spirit to help you.

"Believe in Jesus," Peter said, "and repent, and be baptized for the forgiveness of your sins. You will receive the Holy Spirit too!"

So everyone who heard Peter's words and believed in Jesus was baptized that day—about three thousand people! This was the beginning of the church.

SLEEPY-TIME PRAYER

Dear God, thank You for the Holy Spirit and the power and help He gives us. Good night, God! Amen.

Walking and Leaping

Acts 3–4

Our great power is from God.
—2 Corinthians 4:7 NLT

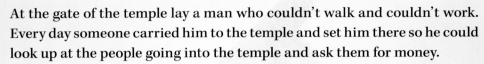

At the gate of the temple lay a man who couldn't walk and couldn't work. Every day someone carried him to the temple and set him there so he could look up at the people going into the temple and ask them for money.

One day, as Peter and John went to the temple to pray, they saw the lame man there. "Could you give me some money, please?" he asked.

"Look at us," Peter said.

The man looked up at Peter and John, expecting them to give him money.

"I don't have any money," Peter said. "But I will give you what I do have. In the name of Jesus Christ of Nazareth, stand up and walk!"

Peter reached out and took the man by the hand to pull him up, and instantly the man's feet and ankles were well! The man jumped up and began to walk! In fact, he walked and leaped right into the temple with Peter and John, praising God. He was so happy to be well!

The people in the temple saw the man walking and leaping. "We've seen this man every day, lying outside the gate, asking for money," they said. "Now he can walk! But how did this happen?" They ran to Peter and John to find out.

Peter talked to the people. "Why are you surprised that this man has been healed?" Peter said. "And why are you staring at us? We

⌐⊸⊸ BEDTIME BLESSING ⊶⊶⌐
Jesus gives you power
to live for Him.

didn't heal the man by any power or goodness of our own. He was healed by the power of Jesus, the One God sent, who died on the cross and was raised again. Jesus is our Savior. Faith in Jesus' name made this man well!"

Many of the people who heard Peter's words believed in Jesus that day and were added to the church.

But some leaders of the people didn't like hearing about Jesus. They arrested Peter and John. "Don't talk or teach about Jesus anymore!" they said.

"Is it right for us to listen to you, or to God?" Peter and John asked. "We can't stop talking about what we have seen and heard!" Then the leaders let them go.

❧ SLEEPY-TIME PRAYER ☙

Dear God, I'm happy for the man who was healed! I want to tell other people what You have done! Good night, God! Amen.

203

Saul's Big Surprise

Acts 9

⚬∽ GOD'S WORDS TO DREAM ON ∽⚬

We can do the good things he planned
for us long ago. —Ephesians 2:10 NLT

Saul, a leader, loved God and worshipped Him. But Saul didn't understand that God had sent Jesus. Saul didn't like Jesus. He didn't like Jesus' followers. He wanted them to stop talking about Jesus. He wanted to hurt them, and sometimes he did.

Saul planned a trip to the city of Damascus. He wanted to arrest Jesus' followers there and put them in prison.

But on the road to Damascus, Saul got a big surprise.

First, he saw a light from heaven, the brightest light he had ever seen—so bright that Saul fell down on the ground.

Then Saul heard a voice. The voice said, "Saul, Saul, why are you hurting Me?"

"Who are You, Lord?" Saul asked.

"I am Jesus, and you are hurting Me when you hurt My followers. Now get up and go into the city, and you will find out what to do next."

Saul got up—but he couldn't see anything. His friends led him into the city to the house where he would stay. For three days he didn't eat or drink.

Jesus told a man named Ananias to go to see Saul.

"But Saul has been hurting Your followers!" Ananias said.

"Go anyway," Jesus said, "because I have important work for Saul to do. I have chosen Saul to tell many people about Me."

So Ananias went to talk to Saul. "Brother Saul," he said, "you saw Jesus on the road to Damascus, and Jesus has sent me here so you can see again and be filled with the Holy Spirit." Suddenly, Saul could see again! He got up and was baptized.

Now Saul had a new life, with a new job—telling others that Jesus was the One God had sent. And Saul got a new name too—he became known to everyone as Paul.

Dear God, thank You for work
to do for You! Help me be a good
worker! Good night, God! Amen.

BEDTIME BLESSING

Jesus has work for you to do.

Praying for Peter

Acts 12

❧ GOD'S WORDS TO DREAM ON ❧

We always pray for you.
—2 Thessalonians 1:11

Herod, a very bad king, didn't like Jesus' apostles teaching the people in Jerusalem about Jesus. Herod arrested Peter and put him in jail.

Then one night, something amazing happened!

While many believers met at Mary's house to pray for him, poor Peter slept in his prison cell with a guard on each side. More guards kept watch at the prison doors. Suddenly, an angel stood in Peter's cell, and light shone all around.

The angel woke Peter. "Get up quickly," the angel said. The chains fell off Peter's hands, but the guards didn't wake up!

"Get dressed and put on your sandals," the angel said. "Then wrap your cloak around you and follow me."

Peter thought he was dreaming, but he did what the angel said. He followed the angel past the guards at the prison doors. Then they came to a heavy iron gate. The gate swung open all by itself, and they walked through the gate into the street. Peter was free!

The angel left. Peter realized that what had happened was real—he wasn't dreaming! "Jesus sent the angel to rescue me!" he said. Then he hurried to Mary's house, knocked on the gate, and called for someone to let him in.

A servant named Rhoda recognized Peter's voice. She was so happy he was free that she forgot to let him in. She ran to tell the others in the house, "Peter is at the gate!"

But they didn't believe her!

"It's true! It's true!" she said. Finally, someone opened the gate—and there stood Peter! He was free, just as the believers had been praying he would be.

"Jesus sent an angel," Peter said. "My chains fell off. The angel led me out of the prison, and here I am! The Lord has saved me!"

⌁ BEDTIME BLESSING ⌁

Jesus hears
and answers prayer.

❧ SLEEPY-TIME PRAYER ❧

Dear God, thank You for listening when I pray.
Thank You for answering prayers the way You
know is best. Good night, God! Amen.

A Young Believer

Acts 16; 2 Timothy 1; 3

❧ GOD'S WORDS TO DREAM ON ❧

"Your word is truth." —John 17:17

Saul became known as Paul, one of Jesus' apostles. He traveled from place to place telling everyone the good news about Jesus and starting new churches. He visited those churches again too, helping the believers stay strong and learn more about God. On one of his trips, Paul traveled to the city of Lystra.

In Lystra, Paul met a young man named Timothy, along with his mother, Eunice, and his grandmother Lois. People in Lystra spoke well of Timothy. "Timothy is a wonderful young man!" they said. "He has great faith even though he is young."

Timothy's mother and grandmother were believers. From the time Timothy was a boy, Eunice and Lois talked with him about what God is like. They read to him from God's Word (just like someone reads Bible stories to you!). And when Timothy got older, he could read God's Word himself.

Timothy had learned that God created the world. He learned that Adam and Eve disobeyed God and that God had promised to send Someone to

BEDTIME BLESSING

The Bible points you
to Jesus.

make things right again. He learned that God planned to bless the whole world through the families of Abraham, Isaac, and Jacob. He learned what is wrong and what is right.

As Timothy grew up and kept reading God's Word, he became wise. When he heard the good news about Jesus, he knew it was true! Jesus was the One God had sent. Timothy became a believer too.

When Paul met Timothy, he could see how much Timothy loved and worshipped Jesus. "Come on my travels with me," Paul said. He knew Timothy would be a good helper and would become a good leader too.

So Timothy began to travel with Paul. They went from place to place, from church to church, helping people live for Jesus everywhere they went.

❧ SLEEPY-TIME PRAYER ❧

Dear God, thank You for the Bible! Thank You that
Your words in the Bible are true. Thank You that I can
hear stories from the Bible and learn to love Jesus,
just like Timothy did. Good night, God! Amen.

Forever with Jesus

1 Thessalonians 4; Revelation 21–22

⊱ GOD'S WORDS TO DREAM ON ⊰

Amen. Come, Lord Jesus!
—Revelation 22:20 ICB

Do you remember that when Jesus went back to heaven, angels told His disciples He would come again someday? It hasn't happened yet, but it will!

Someday Jesus will come back for everyone who believes in Him. He will come from heaven on the clouds, with a loud shout and the sound of a trumpet. Everyone will see Him, and everyone who loves Him will go with Him to live with God forever.

Jesus gave a vision to John the apostle so we can know a little bit of what heaven will be like.

First, heaven will be beautiful. The city of God will come down from heaven to earth, made of pure gold and shining like a jewel. The river of life will flow through the city, and the tree of life will grow beside the river, giving a different kind of fruit for every month. (Do you remember the tree of life from the garden of Eden?)

And heaven will be happy. No one will be sick or sad there. No one will ever cry, and no one will die. God will live with us, and we will see Him face to face. There will be no night because the glory of God and Jesus will give the city its light. Everything will be new! There will never be any trouble, and no one will ever do anything wrong. We will worship God there, and we will rule like kings.

"I am the Alpha and the Omega," Jesus said, "the First and the Last, the Beginning and the End. . . . Yes, I am coming soon!" (Revelation 22:13, 20 ICB).

Yes, come, Lord Jesus!

⌇ SLEEPY-TIME PRAYER ⌇

Dear God, thank You for making everything new. Thank You for making a place where we can live forever with You. Good night, God! Amen.

~ BEDTIME BLESSING ~

Living forever with Jesus
will be wonderful.

Create a Happy
Bedtime Routine

Send your child off to dreamland with a peaceful bedtime routine. Here are some ideas you might find helpful:

- Set your child's bedtime in advance, and maintain it each night as much as possible.

- Choose quiet activities in the hour leading up to bedtime, rather than energetic or competitive games.

- A warm bath or shower helps your child relax. So can brushing her hair or giving him a foot rub.

- A cup of warm milk or cocoa, perhaps with a slice of cinnamon toast, makes a sleep-inducing, comfort-food snack before bed.

- Give gentle reminders of what happens next: "Two more minutes, and then it's time to brush your teeth."

- Keep room lights low while you read, talk, and pray together. You can snuggle together in the child's bed or anywhere quiet where you can sit close. Aim for no distractions; turn off all electronics and put away your phone.

- If you have more than one child, stagger their bedtimes if you can, so they each get one-on-one time with you. Or if you and your spouse each puts one child to bed at the same time, trade off regularly so each child has time with each parent.

- Whatever your routine, follow it well. Children like knowing what to expect.

Tips for Reading with Young Children

Making reading aloud to your child a fabulous experience! Here are some tips to get you started:

- Good stories are made for more than one reading. Children enjoy hearing stories again that they have enjoyed before.

- Don't be shy! Try varying your voice or adding sound effects as you read.

- Pictures help tell the story, often filling in important details. Point to illustrations and talk about them. Invite your child to tell you what's happening in a picture, how a character in an illustration is feeling, or what might happen next.

- Let your child interrupt the story to ask questions.

- Encourage your child to hold the book and turn the pages as you read.

- Try to relate a story to your child's real-world experiences, for example, "Do you remember when our family took a trip?" or, "That donkey looks like the one you rode at the petting zoo."

- Let your child read to you sometimes when he's able. A good way to do this is to take turns reading alternating paragraphs.

About the Author

Diane Stortz is a multipublished author and freelance editor whose heart's desire is for believers to read, learn, love, and live God's Word, the Bible. Popular books include *The Sweetest Story Bible: Sweet Thoughts and Sweet Words for Little Girls*, *A Woman's Guide to Reading the Bible in a Year*, and *I Am: 40 Reasons to Trust God*. She and her husband, Ed, a retired juvenile court probation officer, reside in Cincinnati, Ohio. They have two married daughters and three young grandsons.

Diane cofounded a nondenominational ministry (www.pomnet.org) to help parents of missionaries connect with one another and learn to succeed and thrive as POMs. She coauthored *Parents of Missionaries: How to Thrive and Stay Connected When Your Children and Grandchildren Serve Cross-Culturally.*

When she's not writing or editing, Diane enjoys walking, gardening, and planning her next trip to visit her grandkids.

Visit Diane at DianeStortz.com.

Diane Le Feyer is a French illustrator. Even as a child, she always knew that one day she would draw wonderful pictures for kids to enjoy! She also teaches students what she knows about illustration. Diane is very busy with her life as a teacher, artist, mother, Star Wars enthusiast, and bad cook. She has a darling daughter, a loving husband, and a pearlscale goldfish named Bubbles.